Tales of the Great White

TALES
OF THE
GREAT WHITE

JOCELYN HEANEY

LOWELL HOUSE JUVENILE

LOS ANGELES

NTC/Contemporary Publishing Group

Published by Lowell House
A division of NTC/Contemporary Publishing Group, Inc.
4255 West Touhy Avenue, Lincolnwood (Chicago), Illinois 60712-1975 U.S.A.

Lowell House books can be purchased at special discounts when ordered in bulk
for premiums and special sales. Contact Department CS at the following
address:

   NTC/Contemporary Publishing Group
   4255 West Touhy Avenue
   Lincolnwood, IL 60712-1975
   1-800-323-4900

ISBN: 0-7373-9936-8
Library of Congress Catalog Card Number: 99-71489

Roxbury Park is a division of NTC/Contemporary Publishing Group, Inc.

Managing Director and Publisher: Jack Artenstein
Editor in Chief, Roxbury Park Books: Michael Artenstein
Director of Publishing Services: Rena Copperman
Editorial Assistant: Nicole Monastirsky
Interior Illustrations: Warren Chang
Interior Design: Robert S. Tinnon

Printed and bound in the United States of America
99 00 01 DHD 10 9 8 7 6 5 4 3 2 1

Contents

THE LEGEND OF HARVEY SHANK

The kids at Pacific Middle School can't stop talking about Harvey Shank. Between classes, there are always two or three seventh graders standing by the water fountain in the main hall, whispering a new version of the legend. When they see me coming, they immediately fall silent and walk away, because I alone saw what happened to Harvey, and they know it.

Harvey Shank, Practical Joke King of Pacific Middle School, was serious about only one thing: my best friend, Darcey Parkman, the only person I've ever met who is as much a total marine biology geek as I.

Harvey and I were rivals.

There's really no way that Darcey, a pretty straight-A student, would have ever gone for a delinquent like Harvey Shank —still, I had my doubts. Darcey and I were good friends, but I was a little shy about letting her know *exactly* how I felt about her. Harvey Shank, on the other hand, was anything but shy. He did whatever he wanted to do, no matter what the consequences, particularly if he could get a laugh out of it. In sixth grade, Harvey was expelled for lighting fireworks in the bathroom. A few weeks later, he was banned from St. Bridget's Catholic Church for putting a whoopie cushion inside the confessional. Until the Fishheads camping trip to Stinson Beach last summer, I thought Harvey Shank was invincible.

Darcey and I founded the Fishheads, otherwise known as The Deep Sea Appreciation and Preservation Society. Most kids dropped out when they found out that our advisor, Ms. Brent, required a weekly oral report. They only regular members besides Darcey and me were Mike Ostanopolus, a self-proclaimed expert on plankton, and two irritating twins named Shane and Shawna Pollard, who thought everything in the ocean was boring except moray eels.

Harvey didn't know a manatee from a marlin, but he came to the meetings so Darcey would think he was as obsessed with marine life as we were. He even gave a presentation about the giant squid, although it was obvious he'd copied it straight from an encyclopedia. When the Stinson Beach field trip was announced, Harvey volunteered to help Darcey and Ms. Brent collect permission slips.

Give me a break.

Darcey and I sat together on the school van chartered for the trip. "Do you think Harvey Shank is turning over a new leaf, Phillip?" Darcey asked.

I didn't want to sound jealous, so I gave a fake smile and said, "Stranger things have happened, I guess."

Stinson Beach was located on the northern California coast. Sea lions were in abundance this time of year, and as we left the bus and headed for the beach, Darcey and I saw hundreds of them playing on the craggy rocks of a small island just off shore.

Later that evening, after setting up camp, exploring the tide pools, and listening to Ms. Brent give a talk around the campfire on marine algae, most of us were asleep as soon as our heads hit the pillow—everyone, that is, except Harvey, who crawled into my tent at two in the morning.

"Corbett!" he whispered, lighting the lantern by my bed. "Wake up!"

"Go away, Shank," I mumbled, turning over.

"Want to play cards or something?"

"Why can't you just go to sleep like a normal person?"

"Because I can't," Harvey mumbled. "Not when it's dark."

I sat up. "You're waking me up in the middle of the night to tell me you're afraid of the dark? You're kidding, right?"

Harvey stared into the lantern, adjusting the light. "No."

Something in Harvey's voice made me feel kind of sorry for him. His face looked pale and scared in the glow of the lamp. What can I say? I have a soft heart. I crawled out of my sleeping bag, Harvey grabbed the lantern, and we walked past the cluster of tents down to the beach.

"What's that?" Harvey asked, pointing ahead of us at an object in the sand. Harvey lifted the lantern and the sign came into view: HAZARDOUS CONDITIONS. SWIM AT YOUR OWN RISK.

"What do you think it means?" asked Harvey.

"If you had done your homework, you'd know that the ocean can be dangerous for lots of reasons—strong currents, poisonous fish . . . "

"All right, all right." Harvey reached into his pocket and pulled out a deck of cards. "Wanna play?"

Believe it or not, Harvey and I sort of bonded that night at Stinson Beach. Two weeks later, just before we started seventh grade, Harvey threw a party for the Fishheads at the Oasis Apartments, where he lived.

"The pool is too green and nasty to swim in, so I decided to have a costume party," Harvey explained over the phone.

"I don't know, Shank," I said. "I don't have anything to wear. Besides, I think costume parties are kind of stupid."

"C'mon, Corbett," Harvey wheedled. "Where's your club spirit? What about that fish costume you made for the Marine Biology Fair last year?"

My grouper suit had won first prize. I never though I'd have another chance to wear the costume I'd spent long, agonizing hours creating.

Harvey went on and on about the ocean theme. "My uncle knows a guy who makes plastic body parts for crippled people. He's going to give me a fake leg for my pirate costume. Darcey told me she's coming as a mermaid."

I felt a flash of anger when Harvey mentioned Darcey's name. I had to be there if Darcey was, still I acted hesitant, letting Harvey beg me until I finally agreed.

I retrieved the giant head and swim fins from a box in the garage. August is not the best time of year to be wandering around dressed like a fish, but being hot and sweaty seemed like a small price to pay for having the coolest costume at the party.

My mom dropped me off at Harvey's on her way to the mall. I stumbled across the Oasis Apartments parking lot, peering out of the cut-out eyes, following cardboard signs that read HARVEY'S PARTY. Darcey *was* there, but she was wearing a lime green bikini top and shorts. The pool was blue and clean. Kids dove off the side or sat on the edge, kicking their feet in the shallow end. When Shane Pollard saw me, she laughed so hard she almost dropped her hot dog.

Harvey stood on the diving board, cackling like a hyena. "Nice bathing suit, Corbett," he yelled and jumped high in the air, pulling his legs into his chest and crashing into the center of the pool.

I stood staring at the water, holding the fish head under my arm. I was going to have to take the bus home wearing green tights and swim fins.

I left the party seething with hatred for Harvey Shank.

"Wait up, Phillip! I'll go with you." Darcey ran across the parking lot. "Harvey can be so lame sometimes." She stifled a laugh. "It *is* a great costume, though."

Harvey can be so lame sometimes. Those words sounded like poetry to my ears. Darcey was a saint. She offered to take the bus home with me and even held my dumb fish head in her lap as we sat at the bus stop. We talked about our plans for the club that fall. Darcey wanted to start a campaign to have the school cafeteria serve dolphin-safe tuna. I told her about my latest marine obsession: the strange fish that lived deep in the sea.

"The hatchetfish and lantern fish look transparent, and their organs glow in the dark. There's also this really cool fish called the warted sea devil. It lives at like 600 fathoms and has this little phosphorescent whisker it uses to attract other fish, and . . ."

I was so absorbed with talking to Darcey, that by the time the bus pulled up, I'd forgotten I was dressed like a giant fish.

Harvey didn't attend the school year's first Fishheads meeting. I was sure his stupid fantasies about Darcey had been squashed by the reality of the weekly oral reports. The first assignment Ms. Brent gave us was to write about how different marine animals adapted to their environments. I went to the library to look for a book on deep-sea creatures. It was purely by accident that I discovered great whites.

"*Strange Fish of the Sunless Seas* has been checked out," the librarian said. "But this new book may be of interest to you."

The title was curved inside a set of open jaws. It read: *Great White: The Perfect Predator.* The librarian placed it in my hands.

I sat down in one of the overstuffed library chairs and opened the book to discover awesome things about great whites, like they ram their snouts through the bars of stainless steel cages. *"Each time man enters the ocean,"* the book stated, *"he enters the realm of the fiercest predator on earth."*

Our report was only supposed to be 15 minutes long, but I must have babbled on for at least half an hour. "Every part of the great white shark is designed to make it the perfect predator. The upper teeth are serrated like the edges of steak knives. The dark color of its dorsal side, opposite its white underbelly—which it's named for—helps the shark blend into shadowy kelp beds while it searches for prey swimming above at the surface . . ."

"Thank you, Phillip, that was very informative," Ms. Brent interrupted. "But we must move on to Mike's report on dinoflagellates."

When the time came for the Fishheads to return to Stinson Beach, I begged Ms. Brent to hire shark researchers from the Farallon Islands to take us on a great white expedition. After all, Farallon Islands, known for their large shark population, were only a few miles off Stinson Beach. But Ms. Brent thought the idea sounded too dangerous, so I had to settle on another boring look at tide pools.

The school van was pulling out of the parking lot when out of nowhere Harvey Shank rushed on board. I hadn't spoken to him since the pool party, but Harvey plopped down next to me like we were old friends. Unfortunately, Mike had grabbed the seat next to Darcey, who sat several rows behind us, before I could.

"What are *you* doing here?" I demanded.

"Your fearless leader said I could come as long as I promised to write some stupid report when I get back."

I turned away.

"So, Corbett," Harvey began, "do you think Darcey will ever like me?"

My face flushed. I wanted to say, "Darcey would sooner stick pins in her eyes than look twice at you." But I decided to use a different approach. "Maybe. How much do you like her?"

"A lot." Harvey retrieved a can of grape soda from his lunch bag and popped it open. "I don't know if I ever told you this, but I've liked Darcey ever since I sat behind her in fourth grade."

"Would you be willing to do anything to make her like you?"

"I guess so," Harvey answered uncertainly. "Like what?"

"The first thing you have to understand is Darcey Parkman is not your average girl." The words flowed as effortlessly out of my mouth as if I'd memorized them. "Darcey doesn't have pictures of Leonardo DiCaprio taped up inside her locker. She has pictures of Jacques Cousteau."

"What's your point, Corbett?"

"My point is that Darcey likes adventurers. It's one thing to dare to put a cherry bomb in the school toilet. It's another thing to feel moray eels bite through your wet suit while you're diving off Dangerous Reef. Get it?"

Harvey blew up his empty lunch bag like a balloon. He was just about to pop it when he noticed Ms. Brent glaring at him.

"Yeah, I get it," Harvey mumbled, letting the air out of the bag. "You're saying I don't have a chance."

Neither of us said anything the rest of the way to Stinson Beach.

"Before we begin," Ms. Brent announced, leading us across the empty beach to the tide pools, "I'd like to remind you that your field notebooks must included a detailed drawing and a written description of the life you observe in the tide pools. For those of you who seem to have forgotten your notebooks," she said, staring straight at Harvey, "I will provide paper and a clipboard."

All of us rushed toward the tide pools. Harvey followed Darcey across the rocks, asking if she needed help carrying her school supplies. I wanted to barf.

Mike Ostanopolus found the best tide pool. It was full of crabs and little silver fish. He plunged his hand into the water and retrieved a sea cucumber. It looked more like a rotten egg-plant to me.

"Check it out," Mike said, gently squeezing the sluggish blob, "they can throw up their internal organs." A purple ink-like substance squirted all over his white socks.

My tide pool contained about as much marine life as a mud puddle. It was more interesting to observe how Harvey Shank interacted with his environment. Darcey sat in the shelter of a huge boulder, drawing a piece of kelp while Harvey knelt beside her, sharpening her colored pencils.

"Your drawing looks totally realistic, Darcey."

"Thank you," Darcey answered politely, but I could tell Harvey was starting to irritate her.

"Do you need another color?" Harvey asked, offering her a sea green pencil.

"No thank you, *Harvey*," Darcey replied, pronouncing his name as if she couldn't wait to get it off her tongue.

"Hey, Corbett. Look!" Harvey said, sticking the pencil into the middle of a green anemone. The jellylike mouth closed around the tip. Harvey affected a look of terror. "Help! Help! It's ripping my arm off!"

Darcey sighed, closing her notebook. "I'm going back to the beach," she said, retrieving her pencil box from Harvey. "So I can concentrate."

Harvey watched Darcey walk away along the rocks. The wind whipped his hair into crazy shapes. "What am I going to do, Corbett?" he said. "She hates my guts."

Before I could answer, Mike was pointing to the water, screaming, "Shark, shark!" I jumped to my feet, knocking my notebook into the tide pool. About 30 yards from shore, a black fin was cutting through the waves. I ran as fast as I could down the rocks, my heart racing. Was it possible? Great whites sometimes came close to shore. My heart sank as another fin appeared, then a third, slicing in and out of the water.

"I hate to disappoint you people," said Ms. Brent, walking up from behind us. She was looking through binoculars. "But those ominous fins belong to a pod of dolphins."

"It's hard to tell from far away," Mike said sheepishly.

"Dolphins are boring," Shawna drawled.

"We've seen them a million times at Sea World," said Shane.

Darcey was ecstatic. "May I borrow your binoculars, Ms. Brent?"

"Of course, Darcey," Ms. Brent replied. "Now, if you three find dolphins so incredibly dull, you can help me unpack the water sample kits from the van." She turned to me. "We won't be long, Phillip. Can I trust you and Darcey to keep Harvey out of trouble?"

"Sure." I'd barely heard what she'd said. My eyes were glued to the shifting waves, where the dolphins continued on their journey south.

"You've just got to take a look through the binoculars, Phillip!" Darcey exclaimed and handed them to me.

Looking through the lenses made it seem like I was hovering on the surface of the water. I could almost feel cold foam hitting my face as the dolphins flew past, their bodies shiny and smooth as rubber.

"They're swimming toward the jetty down the beach," I said. "Let's go!"

Darcey and I raced across the cold sand toward the jetty. Anxiously we struggled over the slippery rocks to the tip, only to discover Harvey had gotten there first. Before either of us could say anything, Harvey had taken off his T-shirt and sneakers and dived into the cold dark water. He crashed as clumsily into the Pacific Ocean as he had into the swimming pool at the Oasis Apartments.

Harvey surfaced, waving. "Hey, Darcey! Watch me swim with dolphins!"

"Go get Ms. Brent," I said. "I'll take care of Harvey." I watched Darcey hurry back over the rocks, holding her arms out to the side for balance. Then I turned to Harvey.

"Okay, Shank. Come on out. The joke's over."

The last moments of Harvey Shank's life were, I'm sure he'd agree, quite pleasant. As he thrashed his way in the direction of the long-gone dolphins, he was totally oblivious to the immense shadow gliding toward him from the other direction.

"Shank!"

There was, as it turned out, no time to warn him, because the shark had shifted into attack gear. I stepped up to the tip of the jetty just as Harvey's body exploded from the surface, squeezed between the jaws of a giant shark. I froze. Harvey's screams were muted by the pressure exerted by the powerful creature's bite. All I heard from Harvey's mouth was a horrible gurgling sound. Then the awesome great white took him under.

For a moment, everything was quiet. I remembered something I'd read in the shark book, about how sharks sometimes follow seals and other marine life, waiting for one that lags behind . . .

"We're coming, Phillip!" Ms. Brent called. Her voice sounded faint in the roar and hiss of the ocean. Something rose from the crimson cloud of water. A hopeful voice in my head said: *Harvey got away. He poked the shark in the eyes. He's swimming to the surface, injured but not beyond repair. He's going to need a hundred stitches, but he's going to live.*

Harvey did rise to the surface. Part of him, anyway. The churning water quieted to a gentle sloshing as what was left of Harvey's body rocked back and forth in the bloody foam, like a buoy. Harvey's eyes stared straight ahead, his tattered flesh streaming out from his arms like ribbons.

I don't know what was worse—seeing Harvey's battered corpse afloat in the crimson water or watching the shark pull him beneath the waves for the last time.

Nausea rose in my throat as I staggered across the jetty. It seemed as if a million years had passed since Darcey and I had run across the sand, laughing and carrying on. By the time the others arrived at the jetty, not a trace of Harvey remained.

Each night as I fall asleep, I see Harvey floating in a silent sea. It's not the choppy surf off Stinson Beach. In fact, it doesn't look like any ocean I've ever seen. It must be somewhere past the horizon, a sunless sea where there are no swimmers or boats or fishermen, many fathoms beneath the surface—deeper maybe, than where the great whites swim.

After a few weeks, things settled down at school. The news reporters moved on to some other tragedy, and slowly, day by day, the legend of Harvey Shank was born. He was the boy eaten by a giant squid, strangled by an enormous sea snake, drowned by the ghost of a long-dead pirate . . .

But I alone saw what happened to Harvey Shank, and I'm not talking. That way, the legend will continue to grow. The creatures will become more monstrous and the stories more grotesque. Harvey would have had a good laugh about that.

MAN AND SHARK

The forecast predicted warm, cloudless weather for Monterey. For a weekend vacation with his family, Sheldon Carver—the same Sheldon Carver of the Carver Drive-In chain—had reserved two spacious rooms at the Siete Mares Hotel, each with views of the Pacific Ocean. Sheldon stood on the balcony of one, puffing a cigar and watching the water while his wife, Darlene, and daughter, Tracey, dressed for dinner. The ocean lay dark except for the shimmering tide that curved and broke on the beach. Darlene walked out onto the balcony in a lavender-colored dress.

Tracey followed, dressed in jeans. Sheldon sighed. At least they weren't the faded ultrabaggy ones she wore to school.

The Carvers took the elevator to the four-star restaurant. Everything was perfect, until Sheldon ordered a steak.

Tracey Carver had been a normal kid until she checked out a book on animal rights from the junior high library. Now she could barely walk across the front lawn without worrying about the insects she crushed in the grass. The 14-year-old had stopped wearing leather and given up all red meat, even Sloppy Delights, the Carver Drive-In specialty that had been her favorite food since childhood.

"I guess that makes me a cold-blooded killer," Sheldon snapped after his daughter plastered a MEAT IS MURDER sticker on the bumper of his car.

Sheldon thought Tracey might relax her fanaticism while on vacation. But he had no sooner plunged his fork into the onion-smothered medium-rare T-bone steak than Tracey launched her attack.

"Doesn't it bug you to watch all that blood ooze out?" she grimaced, staring at her father's plate. "Think about it, Dad. Your food had a *face*."

Sheldon carved the tender beef into bite-sized pieces. "I'm not gonna waste too many tears over a big, stupid cow, Tracey. In case you forgot, Miss Bleeding Heart, the evil invention known as the hamburger is funding your college education."

Darlene Carver leaned across the table toward her daughter. "Tracey, please. Remember your father's high blood pressure."

Tracey drizzled honey dressing across her butter lettuce and pear salad. "He probably wouldn't have high blood pressure if he didn't eat all that meat," Tracey muttered. Why did her father have to throw the fortune he'd made from Carver Drive-Ins in her face? It wasn't her fault she was born the daughter of a carnivore. Tracey skewered a pear with her fork and resumed her argument.

"Um, in case you've forgotten, human beings are animals too."

A vein on the side of Sheldon Carver's head started to pulse. "I'll tell you something right now. Man may be an animal, but he doesn't have to live by the same rules as a cow or a fish."

Darlene Carver retrieved a bottle of aspirin from her purse. "I can see this is going to be a long night."

Sheldon continued. "Unlike the rest of his fellow animals, Tracey Ann, man has figured out how to beat Mother Nature at her own game." Sheldon washed down his steak with a gulp of milk. "Man wanted to fly, so he built an airplane. He wanted to swim into the depths of the ocean, so he invented the Aqua-Lung. Man doesn't have one purpose on the earth, he has a thousand. What other animal can send satellites into outer space, compose symphonies or—"

"Start wars," Tracey snapped, "or pollute the environment."

Before Sheldon could reply, a waiter approached the table.

"Enjoying your meal?" he asked.

Darlene smiled. "It's delicious, thank-you."

The Carvers finished their dinner in silence. Sheldon didn't want to argue anymore. Tracey was too immature to see how lucky she was. The modern world had problems, but there was no end to what the human race could accomplish. If a tree was cut down or an alligator made into a pair of shoes in the name of human progress, so be it. Sheldon savored the tender feel of the steak in his mouth. Man was at the top of the food chain. He should be able to enjoy the benefits.

The next morning, Sheldon was determined to put his argument with Tracey behind him and enjoy the rest of the week-end. At eight in the morning, he roused his daughter from a sound sleep.

"Come on, lazy bones," he said, "we're all going out to breakfast."

Tracey groaned and put her pillow over her head. "C'mon, Dad. You're the one who said we were on vacation. It's *so* early. Can't I sleep in?"

"I thought you did all your sleeping in school," Sheldon chuckled.

Tracey made a disgusted face under her pillow. Her father was such a dork sometimes.

Sheldon Carver dragged his groggy wife and daughter to a beachfront cafe called the Sunflower. "You'll like this place, Tracey," Darlene offered. "The menu says they use only natural ingredients in their food."

Tracey yawned. "I'm sure it's fine, Mom."

Sheldon made one last effort to ease the tension around the breakfast table. "I hope no oats suffered in the making of your granola," he teased, swabbing up the maple syrup from his plate with his soy sausage.

"Ha, ha," Tracey mumbled, poking at her cereal with a spoon.

"Come on, honey, lighten up," Sheldon exclaimed. "You're too young to carry the weight of the world on your shoulders. I don't want to spend the whole weekend arguing." Sheldon looked at his empty plate. The whole-wheat pancakes he'd ordered had been OK, but the soy sausage tasted like sawdust.

Several times throughout the meal, Sheldon had gazed across the street to the Egg Parlor Coffee Shop. He could smell the scent of bacon, greasy hash browns, and real sausage. But he'd pretended to enjoy his health food breakfast for Tracey's benefit. Besides, if they'd eaten at the Egg Parlor, Darlene would've nagged him about not ordering sausage because of his high cholesterol.

"So what do you say we all go to the beach after breakfast?" Sheldon asked, paying the check.

"Oh, that sounds wonderful," Darlene exclaimed. "Tracey loves to swim, don't you, Tracey?"

Tracey sighed. "Sure."

"All right then," Sheldon rose from the table. "Shall we?"

It had been one month since the great white shark had eaten. Its last prey had been a juvenile elephant seal, north of Monterey near the Farallon Islands. With their quick, agile leaps and dives through the water, seals often eluded great whites, but this young mammal had not been aware of the shark's presence until it was too late. Cruising the kelp beds on the ocean floor, the shark had spotted the seal silhouetted along the surface. The great white had risen slowly at first and then rushed upward, body curved and jaws parted to tear a huge chunk of flesh from the seal's stomach. The disemboweled creature flew out of the water in an explosion of foam, its agonized barks echoing across the island's rocky shore.

The great white hovered beneath the surface as the dying seal's blood flooded the sea. When its prey ceased to struggle, the shark struck again. In one quick motion, the great white yanked the seal beneath the waves. The shark shook its head violently back and forth like a dog with a toy, its teeth slicing into the seal's thick, fatty hide.

Now the shark was hungry again. On its journey south from the Farallons, it had followed a pod of dolphins for a half mile or so but, wary of their numbers, did not attack. It had grazed the bottom of a deep-sea fishing boat, attracted by the electro-magnetic fields emitted by a ladder on the ship's side. But circling beneath the boat a few times, nudging the ladder with its snout, the animal failed to find edible prey. So it glided away, unnoticed by the fishermen on board. As the noon sun flecked the surface of the Pacific with light, the great white turned away from the open ocean and swam toward shallow water.

Sheldon didn't really like to swim, but he wanted to get his money's worth from the vacation. It seemed wasteful to return from a weekend at the beach without having ever been in the water.

Darlene said she and Tracey would join him at the beach. Tracey wanted to find a store that sold sunblock that wasn't tested on animals.

Sheldon went back to the hotel to shower and shave. Scientists could clone a sheep, but no one had yet invented a nick-proof razor. The cut was deep enough to require two Band-Aids. Sheldon applied them to his neck so they formed an X. He then opened his suitcase and grabbed a beach towel emblazoned with the logo of Carver Drive-In. Sheldon had designed the logo himself: a smiling Sloppy Delight with a top hat and cane. Beneath the dancing chili burger was the invitation: COME TO CARVER'S FOR A MEATY TASTE TREAT.

The beach was crowded. Sheldon stepped carefully over the tan, fit bodies that covered the sand. He tried not to be embarrassed by the excess flesh that jiggled over the waistband of his swim trunks. Darlene was absolutely right. He did need go on a diet. But after working so hard, didn't a man deserve to reward himself a bit?

Sheldon found his family on a little slope of sand near the water's edge. Darlene was reading a mystery novel. Tracey was rubbing sunscreen on her arms and listening to music on her portable CD player. Every time Sheldon tried to talk to her, Tracey pulled the earphones away from her ears with an irritated "*What?!*"

Sheldon quit trying to communicate with his daughter and spread his towel on the sand. He smeared his pale body with the remainder of the waterproof sunblock.

The ocean looked calm and flat as a swimming pool. A group of children hopped in and out of the tide. A teenage boy ran past the children, chasing a large Labrador retriever. Sheldon saw that the dog carried a dead seagull in its mouth. The bird's neck was broken, and its useless head lolled to one side as the dog trotted along the shoreline. *I wish Tracey could see that*, Sheldon thought. *Maybe then she'd realize man isn't the only cruel animal in the world.* Sheldon looked over at his daughter, but Tracey lay facedown on her beach towel, fast asleep.

"Well, I guess I'll be the first to venture in," Sheldon said.

"You'd better take a couple of antacid tablets so you don't get a cramp," Darlene cautioned without raising her eyes from her book.

"Oh, I'll be fine, " Sheldon grumbled.

Sheldon waded cautiously into the water. It was bitingly cold. No wonder he never went into the ocean.

Sheldon stood in the shallow water, shivering for a few moments, then determinedly threw himself in, hitting the water with a wet splat. An icy current coursed through his body. His head ached.

Sheldon rose above the water, taking gasps of air through his open mouth. Keeping his head above the surface, Sheldon pulled himself through the ocean in a frantic, clawing version of the dog paddle. So focused was he on staying afloat, he didn't notice when the bandages fell away from his neck and the warm trail of his blood drifted into the current.

Besides the two remora fish attached to its snow-white underbelly, the shark swam alone. It moved through the water at a slow, effortless pace, guided by the sensations detected in its Y-shaped brain and kept buoyant by the water in its liver and the oxygen flowing through its two-chambered heart.

The great white had no reason to increase its speed. It had no natural enemies in the sea. If it spotted a seal, fish, or even a sea bird alighting on the surface, it could accelerate suddenly, driven forward by a few snakelike motions of its tail. The rough sandpaper denticles, or projections, of its skin—themselves like teeth—increased the flow of water across the shark's body, while decreasing the sound of its movement through the water, allowing it to approach its prey silently.

The shark's body temperature was much higher than that of the ocean. The animal was therefore unaffected by the chill of the water that flowed over the gray armor of its flanks. It was aware only of the scent of an injured animal. It was able to detect one part of blood in a million parts of water. The shark flexed its two side fins, adjusting its course as it swam toward the scent of food.

Sheldon was about 50 yards from the beach when the cramp tore through his stomach. He thought of Darlene, warning him about swimming too soon after eating. If he squinted, he could see his wife on the shore. She stood on the beach, shading her eyes and looking out toward the ocean. Sheldon tried to wave to her, but another cramp ripped through his abdomen. He grabbed his stomach with his hand. It felt like a spiked ball was rolling through his lower body. Sheldon closed his eyes and paddled, half sinking, half swimming toward the beach. His breathing came in short gasps.

The shark did not recognize as a man the oddly shaped animal that lurched through the water. Sharks had been swimming in the ocean one hundred times longer than had human beings. It could be argued that man was the great white's only enemy in the world, but even men remained strangers in the shark's underwater world. The fish approached the pale, floundering body with the same stealth as if Sheldon Carver had been a wounded seal or a dolphin.

Sheldon saw only a flash of white, as if a bolt of underwater lightning had thrown him from the sea. In his panic, he thought the sudden explosion of pain in his abdomen meant that his appendix had burst. Then he realized whatever had caused the pain in his stomach was pulling him beneath the waves. He was drowning and bleeding to death at the same time. Water filled his mouth. Sheldon Carver tasted his own blood as the shark's teeth sank into his soft flesh.

As the animal fought against death, the shark waited motion-lessly. Once its prey stopped struggling, the great white returned, driven neither by mercy nor cruelty. It followed only the instinct that had guided its kind since before there were dinosaurs on the earth. Or trees. With one quick twist of its tail, the great white shark fulfilled its purpose.

SHARK BOY

When he was three years old, Henry Price fell into the sea. He and his mother were sailing the Indian Ocean on a cruise ship. The very first night a fire, starting in one of the cabins, raged onboard. Henry was pulled by his mother from his bed to join the frantic passengers swarming to the deck. Men and women dressed in their pajamas and bathrobes pushed and shoved one another as they crowded into overflowing lifeboats. Panicking, people leaped overboard.

A light rain fell. Hugging Henry close, his mother scanned the desperate faces. Suddenly a man grabbed her hand. She turned to see a kind, weathered face framed by white hair. "Come with me," the man urged. "There's enough room for you and your son in this raft I found on board. But we must hurry."

The man's name was Carson. Carson held Henry as his mother descended the ladder on the side of the ship to a small yellow raft. "Thank you," she murmured as Carson gently handed her the boy. She smoothed Henry's hair. "We owe you our lives." Carson looked at the woman. Her thick black hair covered the child's face.

Carson smiled. "Yes, you're safe now," he said. He took the oars and guided the raft away from the ship.

The dark sea was a chaos of boats and bodies, illuminated by the orange glow of the burning ship. Survivors swam toward one another in the dark, now and then bumping into the charred bodies of the dead that floated in the sea. Wind whipped across the sea's surface, carrying the smell of smoke and burned flesh. Lifeboats tossed uncertainly about on the growing swells.

With no warning, the rain surged into a downpour, extinguishing the fire that consumed the ship and shrouding the sea in blackness. Then the sharks came.

A school of white tip sharks arrived first, nudging the drowned bodies with their noses. Some left after this initial inspection. Others circled those stranded in the water, terrified as the sharks tore limbs off the burned and bloated corpses. With no other refuge, they huddled together, treading water. When a fin surfaced nearby, someone would scream "Shark! Shark!" and the group would slap the water with their hands until the fish sped away. This tactic worked unless a shark approached unseen from below and yanked one of them down into the sea.

White tips were not the only sharks in the South African waters. As Carson fought to keep the raft afloat on the 15-foot swells, he noticed a flash of gray and white rise from the stormy sea. Carson leaned over the side of the raft for a closer look when a wave crashed against the craft, tossing its occupants into the ocean.

"Henry!" Carson could not see the boy's mother, but he heard her calling for her son over the wail of the wind. Carson was sure the boy had drowned, until he heard Henry crying for his mother. Carson swam hurriedly in the direction of the cries just in time. Water was filling the child's mouth as he struggled to keep his head above the churning waves.

Beyond the child's bobbing shadow, Carson saw his mother. The sea would soon claim her. Realizing she was beyond hope, Carson reached out and put his arm around Henry, pulling the boy close to him. Together they reached the overturned raft and—at least for now—safety.

Henry kept his face buried in Carson's chest, as they huddled together in the raft. He didn't see his mother die. But Carson witnessed the gray and white shark rise out of the oily darkness and take her before she had time to scream.

Carson and Henry drifted in the Indian Ocean. The first day, Henry called out for his mother, but after that, his own hunger and thirst consumed him. The next day, in the evening, they were blessed with rain. Carson unfolded a tarpaulin stored there in the raft and with it collected water for them to drink. Henry drank first, gathering the water in his small, cupped hands.

When the water was gone, hunger still remained. Then, on the third day, as they drifted in the sweltering heat, Henry suddenly grabbed Carson's arm. He pointed toward the water. There was a sea turtle, paddling next to the raft. Without missing a beat, Carson successfully speared the animal with a knife he'd brought with him from the ship.

The two ate some of the meat raw, leaving the rest to dry on the floor of the raft. The turtle's blood, Carson drained onto the tarpaulin. He and the boy drank it as eagerly as if it had been cold spring water.

Four days later, the raft drifted lazily into the lagoon of the tiny island of Baku. Henry's face was covered with heat blisters, and he was alarmingly dehydrated. Carson, delirious, was close to death.

A native fisherman named Timu found the raft and towed it to shore. In the village, women applied cool, wet cloths to Henry's body. A group of villagers gathered around Carson and tried to revive him by pouring water on his lips.

Carson slept in Timu's house that afternoon and well into the next day. He woke long enough to take sips of water or eat bits of fruit. When he found strength enough to speak, he leaned over to Timu and whispered "Do you speak English?"

"Yes."

"Where is the boy?"

"He is sleeping," Timu said.

Timu had learned a little English from the men who came to Baku to harvest timber from the lush jungle. Many of the islanders who worked in the lumber camps could write and speak English almost perfectly. These people called themselves islanders, but they had no real loyalty to the ancient ways. Timu resented the outsiders too much to become fluent in their language. Still, he understood most of Carson's story, linking together words he recognized.

Carson paused a moment, taking a slow, painful breath. "The boy's name is Henry," he continued in a voice like dry leaves. "I know nothing else about him. His mother is gone. A shark took her the night the ship went down." Timu offered Carson a wooden cup filled with water. Carson leaned up on his elbow and drank.

Then he drifted back to sleep. "I know I am dying. I have already accepted it. Henry is young. He is alone in the world. He will have no one when I am gone." Carson's eyes closed. He fell back into the dream state somewhere between sleep and death.

Timu sat by the man's bed for a long time. He watched Carson sleep and thought about his words. Could it be true? The island legends said that if the native people were ever in trouble, the sacred shark race would return to Baku. As in the ancient tales, the boy's mother had been of the shark race, but had given up her son to the world of men. The dying man was wise. He'd given the boy the blood of the sea turtle to drink, the same thing the shark race consumed to give them the courage of warriors.

Timu had prayed for the return of the Blessed Race. Each day, the outside world seemed to invade Baku more and more. When Timu was young, children of the island were content to play in the jungles and listen to the stories the elders told after the evening meal. Now many of them dreamed of living in crowded cities where the air was dirty, watching television and driving cars.

When the shark race returned, the outsiders would be driven away. The jungles and seas would replenish themselves, and the Baku islanders would remember how to be a strong, united people.

Timu discussed Carson's story with the village elders. The council decided Timu would raise Henry as his son. When the boy turned 12 he would leave the village and live for one year with the holy men in the mountains. There Henry would fast and meditate, learning how to summon the powers of the shark race in his meditations. He would return to the village a warrior.

Henry grew up feeling like a citizen of two worlds; the island of Baku and a place he could not remember, a country beyond the horizon and across the sea.

"Probably America," Timu said, "but I do not know." Henry called Timu "Father," although he knew that Timu was not the man who'd brought him into the world or given him his name. Timu told Henry all he knew of the boy's origins.

"I will always call you 'Henry' because this is the name you were given by the man who saved your life. You were ill. The man was dying. I tried to understand everything the man told me, although sometimes he spoke like someone dreaming with his eyes open."

Next to Timu, Kali was the closest person to Henry. Kali was the same age as Henry. They did everything together. Kali showed Henry how to make traps to catch the tiny yellow fish that swam in the lagoon. Henry and Kali hid in the trees near the lumber camp and threw rocks at the workers. But as the boys got older, their curiosity grew about the men their elders told them to hate. A man named Pete let Kali and Henry take pictures of each other with a Polaroid camera. Henry loved to hold the undeveloped pictures in his hand and see the images slowly come to life.

"This is a good way to practice English," Pete said, handing Henry and Kali a superhero comic book. The boys thought the lumbermen were pretty nice for outsiders. As the two walked home through the jungle, one of them would slowly decipher the adventures of the X-Men or Batman out loud to the other, resuming the native dialect when they neared the village.

Timu was angry when he discovered the comic books Henry had hidden behind the house. Timu believed the lumbermen were as bad an enemy as the pirates who'd raided Baku hundreds of years before. "They destroyed our land and replaced our sacred stories with their silly books," Timu griped.

As much as Timu complained, some of the old traditions remained. Each night at dusk, the fishermen returned to the village and gave their catch to the women. The women wrapped the fresh fish in green leaves to give it a smoky flavor when it was roasted over the fire. Once the meal was done, the elders took turns telling stories.

One night when Henry and Kali were very young, Kali's father told a story that explained the significance of the trees harvested by the men in the lumber camps.

"The outsiders have their own special name for the trees they cut down. But we call them ghost trees because they are inhabited by the spirits of the island ancestors." Kali took a drink of the palm wine passed to him in a large cup.

"The twisted trunks are inhabited by the wise men who died when they were very old. Their spirits bend the trees toward the ground. If you should walk through the forest where some trees still stand, you will notice some that stopped growing when they were still quite small. These trees are also sacred. They house the spirits of those who died young, infants born dead and children who drowned in the sea. Sometimes, at night, when a breeze moves through the branches, you can hear the children crying in the wind."

Kali's father passed the wine to Timu. This meant it was his turn to tell a story. The villagers knew Timu liked to talk. Especially when he'd drunk a little wine.

"Baku islanders were not always the brave, intelligent race we are today, " he began. The villagers laughed.

"The first inhabitants of the island—we call the Original People—did not live in harmony with their neighbors. They were terrible warriors and fishermen. When outsiders came to make war on them, they fled to the jungle, allowing their enemies to rob their villages. Although the seas were plentiful, the Original People knew nothing of the ways of animals. Fish, rays, and turtles swam past their nets.

"Safi was a fisherman who feared his people were destined to be killed by outsiders or else starve to death. He journeyed to the mountains and made an offering of fish to the spirits at one of the holy shrines. Fish was a priceless gift, and Safi wanted the spirits to take his prayers seriously. He asked the spirits to give the Baku islanders two gifts: the strength of warriors and the wisdom of animals.

"The next day, as Safi stood knee deep in water, casting his nets in the lagoon, he saw a shark. The fisherman had seen blue sharks and copper-colored sharks, but this fish was different. It had a thick gray body and moved very slowly through the water. The water was clear enough for Safi to see the black tips on the bottom of its fins. The shark swam straight toward him, but he was not afraid. The fish was female, its belly heavy with babies. The shark swam into the shallows until her fins dragged on the sandy bottom. For a moment, Safi wondered if the fish was ill and was throwing herself on the shore until she suffocated in the air.

"Instead, the shark used her fins to push herself onto the shore. Little by little, as the strange fish emerged from the sea, her fins turned into arms and her tail became legs that carried her across the sand. Her gills grew into long dark hair. Her body became human. The shark rose from the sea, a beautiful woman.

"The shark woman gave birth to two sons. They resembled normal human boys, except they had the power to return to their former shape when they entered the sea. At first, the islanders watched the transformation of the shark boys with wonder, but soon this event became as common as watching a man gather his net from the sea. Even the children took no notice of it. But I will describe it to you, since we have seen nothing like it in our time.

"When the shark boys tired of playing games in the jungle, they would race each other to the sea. They ran into the water on legs, but as soon as they plunged into the ocean, their bodies would dissolve. If you looked at the water, you might see a black shadow, then a tail fin cut the surface. The shark boys would chase each other around the lagoon for a while, until they swam off to explore secret places in the sea that no human being has ever seen.

"The shark boys taught the fishermen how to stand very quietly on the rocks and cast their nets before the fish sensed their presence. It is said that this shark power has stayed with the Baku islanders ever since, which is why we do not have trouble catching food from the sea."

Timu drank the rest of his wine. He nudged Henry, who dozed in the warm glow of the fire. Henry opened his eyes for a moment, then resumed his slumber.

"When the boys reached the end of childhood, they were ready to become warriors. Their mother sacrificed a sea turtle and let her sons drink the animal's blood. 'Just as this animal has sacrificed its life, so have you relinquished your animal nature to live in the world of men,' she explained. 'Although you will retain the wisdom of the sea creatures, now that you have tasted the drink of warriors, you will never be able to return to your former shape.'"

The villagers listened intently to the end of the story, all except Henry, who was fast asleep.

"The shark woman then bid farewell to her sons. The boys watched her walk into the sea, her limbs and hair disappearing slowly into the water as she changed from woman to fish.

"Her sons were such fierce warriors, the islanders' enemies came to fear them and no longer started wars against them. The shark race lived on Baku until they were very old men, teaching the islanders the ways of the sea and its creatures.

"If we catch a shark in our nets, we do not kill it out of respect for this gift. It is said that if the islanders are ever in trouble again, if the sea runs out of fish or if our enemies return, the shark woman will send us another of her children."

Timu finished the story. Everyone was quiet for a few moments. Kali whispered to Henry to wake up.

"You missed the best parts," Kali said.

Henry rubbed his eyes. "No, I didn't. I was awake."

"Then tell me the story," Kali challenged.

Henry stared dreamily into the fire. "There were these two boys. Their mother was a shark, only she could walk on land. The boys could turn into sharks only if they went swimming—"

Kali laughed. "I think you left out a few parts, Henry."

Henry didn't remember the details of the ancient story, but sometimes, when he looked out at the water, he imagined what it would feel like to leave behind the human world forever. Henry thought of how good it would feel to slip into the water and swim until his arms became fins, until he no longer thought in words but only felt the cold water rush against his body.

Henry did not think about the gift the shark race gave to the Original People until he and Kali, now 12 years old, prepared to go on the Quest for the Animal Guide. Every boy on Baku looked forward to his turn at the quest, since it meant he had officially become an adult.

Each spring, village boys embarked on the quest, a three-day ceremony during which they sought out their dream animal. Tribal elders took the boys deep into the jungle, where they would fast and meditate for two days until the vision of their dream animal came to them. When the boys returned to the village the next day, the elders held a feast for them on the beach. After the feast, the boys danced and played games. The elders would then interpret each boy's vision. His dream animal represented something about the boy's character that determined what position he would hold in the village.

"I hope I don't see a wild boar," Kali told Henry as they climbed on rocks near the lagoon. "My father says boars are the worst guide animal to have. They're strong but stupid. A boar man would never make a good warrior."

Henry threw a smooth black stone into the sea. "I want to see a shark," Henry said. "The elders say seeing a shark means you will receive messages from the ancestor spirits."

Kali looked at his friend strangely. "But why would a shark mean anything to you, Henry? *Our* ancestors are not the same as *your* ancestors."

The two boys walked the entire way back to the village in silence. Kali's words hurt Henry because Henry knew they were true. No matter how close Henry felt to Timu or to Kali, Henry felt quite certain he would always be viewed as an outsider.

Henry and Kali parted ways at the clearing. Kali took the path home through the jungle. Henry followed a trail that wound around the beach and led to his house. Timu sat on a small wooden bench just outside the front door, mending a torn fishing net.

"Father," Henry asked, "what was your animal guide?"

"A lizard," Timu replied, testing the strength of the net between his hands. "I always thought I should have been a monkey, because I never shut up."

Henry laughed, thinking of his father's love of telling stories. "Do you think it is possible to tell what a boy's spirit guide is just by looking at him?"

Timu frowned. "If a boy has a special destiny, holy men often see the shadow of the dream animal behind him as he walks. Why do you ask, Henry?"

Henry paused. He didn't know how to put the loneliness he felt into words without hurting Timu. "You have given me a good life, Father. But I have always felt different because I was not born on the island. I know the ceremony is only a week away, but I thought that if I knew what my animal guide was beforehand, I might understand . . . more about who I am."

Timu remained quiet for several moments. "There is much I must tell you, Henry." He motioned for the boy to sit next to him on the bench. "It does not matter what your spirit animal is. The ancient laws demand that only children born on Baku participate in the quest. You are no less my son because of this, but you will always be different because you arrived here from another place."

Henry's face flushed with humiliation. "But father, if I don't go on this quest, I will remain a boy in the eyes of the villagers."

Timu put his hand on Henry's shoulder. "You will not remain a child, Henry." Timu stared toward where the light filtered through the tangled trees. "In some ways, you never were. I have told you how you arrived at the island with a man in a yellow boat. Your mother gave you to him before she returned to the sea. When you were still a child, he nourished you with the food of the shark ancestors. When the man died, we buried him in the grove of the ghost trees to honor him for bringing you to us. He kept you alive with food and water, but I believe the shark ancestors guided your boat to the island." Timu stared into Henry's eyes. "They gave you to me as a gift."

Henry smiled nervously. An hour before, Henry had hoped to receive a message from the shark ancestors. Now that Timu told him he was the son of a shark, he had to stifle his laughter.

"I'm sorry, Father. It is just hard for me to believe . . . I mean, those old stories . . . are just stories, aren't they?"

Timu failed to share Henry's amusement. "It was prophesied that the shark race would return if we ever needed help. Look around you, Henry. The very land where your guardian is buried is being destroyed. We are no longer raided by pirates, but our people have lost their warrior spirits. They do not know how to fight against these new enemies. Now that you've turned 12, things will change." Timu placed his hands on Henry's shoulders. "Don't you understand? I have prayed for you to come."

Henry stared at the ground. "But, Father, I don't feel like a warrior. I still feel like a child."

"Of course." Timu smiled. "That is why it is not enough for you to go on a boy's quest. You will go to the mountains and live among the holy men. Only then will your true, warrior nature be revealed to you. You will save us, Henry. It will be a difficult life, but an honorable one."

Henry nodded. "Yes, Father."

"Don't worry, Henry," Timu said. "Even if you don't feel like a warrior yet, know you have the spirit inside you. Listen to that spirit. Let it guide you."

Henry lay in bed, listening to the croaking of the tree frogs. The sound that usually comforted Henry as he drifted off to sleep tonight agitated him. But even if the jungle had been perfectly silent, Henry doubted he could have ever fallen asleep.

Overnight, his childhood had vanished. He carried the responsibility of the entire island on his shoulders. The same questions raced through his mind over and over: Why must he be responsible for the fate of Baku when he wasn't even born there? Timu was not his real father—why should he submit to this man's beliefs? How could he ever rid the island of outsiders when those people had shown him only kindness? Perhaps he belonged more to them than he did to the island.

There had to be a way to escape. Henry stayed up night after night. He considered running off to the jungle, finding some unexplored part of the island, and hiding there.

He also considered asking one of the men from the lumber camp to take him aboard ship and set sail for some far-away place: Europe or America. Even if none of the men agreed, he could stow away. But what would he do once he came ashore? He was only 12 years old. He had no idea what life was like beyond the island.

Henry took long walks around the lagoon. He asked the spirit world for a sign, but none came to him. Henry would have no choice but to accept his fate.

As the days passed, Kali and the other village boys prepared to leave on their quest. Henry watched from the edge of the jungle as the boys formed two lines in the middle of the village. They laughed and shoved one another, but when the tribal elders came to lead them into the forest, the boys fell silent and stood as rigid as soldiers. Henry watched as they marched down the winding path that led away from the village. Henry was so deep in thought, he was startled by the feeling of Timu's hand on his arm.

"You don't have time to be jealous, Henry," Timu said. "You have too much work to do. In three days, you will leave for the mountains. Before you see the holy men, you must first purify yourself."

In preparation for his fast, Henry had eaten only a few small pieces of fruit that morning, washed down with water. That evening, Timu stayed at the house of a friend in the village, leaving Henry alone to meditate.

Henry followed Timu's instructions. He lit two candles and burned bundles of leaves, letting the clean smoke drift through the open window. He then sat on a mat in the center of the room and waited for a vision to come to him.

At first Henry was aware only of the rumbling in his stomach. His thoughts wandered to the boys on their quest. He wondered if Kali was having as much trouble concentrating on a vision. He decided to forget about his hunger by falling asleep.

The next morning and afternoon, Henry repeated the meditation. On the evening of the second day, just when Henry started to believe there were no such things as visions, the woman came to him.

At first, Henry thought he must have fallen asleep while meditating, but everything felt too real to be a dream. Henry saw himself walking along the shore. He could feel the hard, cold sand under his feet and smell the salt of the sea. A woman walked toward him. She was not someone Henry recognized from the village, yet she was familiar to Henry in a way he could not describe. The moon illuminated her face. Her long hair moved in the slight, warm breeze. Just when Henry was on the verge of remembering her, the image of the woman faded from his mind. The next day, she entered Henry's meditation again. This time she smiled and put out her hand. Henry took it. They walked together to the water.

The village boys returned to the beach the next evening. Mothers rushed out of their homes and welcomed their sons. The village elders prepared for the feast by slaughtering a wild boar at the edge of the water.

When Timu returned home that evening, Henry was thinking of the woman in his vision.

"You may eat tonight, Henry," Timu said. "Your fast is ended."

"No thank you, Father."

Henry was afraid that if he ate he would not be able to receive another vision. He told Timu he was too tired to go with him to the feast. Instead, he stayed home, watching the glow of the fires through the trees, listening to the voices and laughter echo through the jungle. In the morning he would leave the village and go live in the mountains. Feelings of loneliness returned.

He listened until the sounds of celebration died away. Timu returned and went to bed. The island was silent except for a chorus of unseen insects and birds. Henry closed his eyes. He was delirious with hunger, but he finally understood. The visions had shown him. His loneliness had come from living too long in the world of men. Henry was a shark boy. He belonged to the Blessed Race. Why else had the woman wanted Henry to follow her to the water? Timu's words returned to him: *Listen to the spirit. Let it guide you.*

Henry walked to the beach. The full moon flooded the lagoon. The air smelled like smoke, from the torches burned at the feast. The night felt just the same as in his vision. Henry looked down the beach for the long-haired woman. He wondered if she already waited for him in the sea. The water, stained with the dark red blood of the sacrificed animals, felt warm against his skin.

The white shark swam a few feet below the surface. The scent of blood that led it to the lagoon was now accompanied by a thrashing motion. The shark turned toward the shadow that swam across the moon-bright sea.

Henry's last thought was that he'd returned to his original form. He could feel his human soul passing out of his body with his breath. It was as if his mind had been severed from his body, as if he had passed into an altered state of being, somewhere between the shark's existence and his former self. There was no pain. Henry felt only great pressure as he became a shark once more. The great white's jaws closed and crushed Henry's bones. The shark's teeth pierced his heart again. Henry had no more thoughts, but for a brief moment was conscious of the sea that swirled around him and the moon burning like cold fire. Then he returned to the dark water from which he'd come.

SHADOW IN THE WAVES

Before Heartson's Pond even froze, Sarah's friends, Haley and Carmen, talked about racing across it on their skates, spinning and laughing, executing perfect figure eights. Sarah pictured herself crashing through the thin ice and drowning in the frigid water.

Sarah kept such crazy fears to herself. Someone finding out that Sarah Marie Miller, the daughter of a Harvard graduate, and winner of the Corn Belt Middle School Outstanding English student award, was, in fact, a total chicken, terrified Sarah more than all her phobias combined. Instead, she weaseled out of things that scared her by playing it cool.

"I'd rather go roller-skating than ice skating," she'd remark casually to Haley and Carmen. "At least you can listen to music at the rink." Of course, the only time Sarah had ever tried to roller-skate, she'd barely stood up before she'd fallen on her butt in the middle of the rink. Then when struggling to her feet, she split her pants open in front of half the fifth grade class.

If her friends actually agreed to go to the rink, Sarah would make some other excuse. "You guys go ahead. I think I'll stay home and finish reading this book my father lent me. Have you ever heard of it? It's called *Catcher in the Rye* by J. D. Salinger."

Haley shrugged. "Sounds pretty boring."

Carmen sighed. "Leave it to the library geek to flake out on us again."

Sarah accepted the role of bookworm if it meant escaping a more serious humiliation. "I know," Sarah said. "I'm just an egghead."

Then at the end of Sarah's seventh grade year, her parents made plans she couldn't possibly flake out on.

"Honey," her mother informed Sarah one morning over breakfast, "your father has been offered a professorship at U.C. San Diego. I know it's kind of sudden, but don't worry. You'll be able to finish out the school year at Corn Belt. We're not moving until early July."

Sarah felt a familiar adrenaline surge of fear. *California?* All she could picture was girls wearing bubble gum-pink bikinis to class. Sarah would look like a bag lady in her long flowered skirts and scuffed penny loafers. *Everyone will hate me*, she thought.

"But, Mother, can't Father find a job at a college in Nebraska? California is so . . . *far away*."

"May I remind you how much a certain 13-year-old girl who shall remain nameless complains about Nebraska winters?" Her mother leaned over Sarah and sliced bananas into her cereal bowl. Sarah hated it when she did that. It made her feel like a little child.

"I believe this is a direct quote: 'Harmon is a boring town, and most of my classmates are stupid hicks?'" Her mother threw the banana peel in the trash. "Why don't you try to think of San Diego as a new start?"

Sarah glared at her cornflakes. Her mother was right. But why did Harmon, Nebraska, suddenly seem like the greatest town in America?

From the moment the flight attendant told her to place her tray table in an upright, locked position to the time the plane landed in San Diego, Sarah gave an Oscar-winning performance in bravery. Or at least she tried to.

"Are you OK, honey?" her father asked, when his daughter returned from the bathroom for the third time. Sarah had refused his offer of nausea pills, but she was convinced she'd hurl airplane food all over her lap if they encountered any more turbulence.

"I'm fine, Father." Sarah eased herself slowly into her seat. "I was just checking to see if they have anything to read back there besides golf magazines."

When Sarah stepped off the plane in San Diego, she felt like she had landed on Mars. The sun burned hot on her shoulders. Then, while her father nervously navigated the 405 freeway in the Millers' rented car, instead of cornfields stretching out on either side of country roads, she saw malls and Spanish-style homes sprawling along the highway.

Outside of the rolling grasslands, Nebraska was flat. In California, huge mountains sloped down to the sea and disappeared in fog. Palm trees towered over wide streets. Kids rode skateboards on the sidewalk.

The Millers' house smelled like fresh paint and new carpet. Sarah had barely started unpacking her books when her mother bounced into her room. "You can finish that later, Sarah. Get your suit on. We're going to the beach."

"You know I hate swimming, Mother."

"This isn't Heartson's Pond, Sarah. Don't you want to send a postcard to Haley and Carmen and tell them you've actually felt the Pacific Ocean on your skin? You don't have to actually swim. Just go in up to your waist."

"It's not like I'm *afraid*," Sarah snapped. "I just want to stay here and get unpacked."

An hour later, Sarah was trudging across the beach after her parents with a tube of sunscreen under one arm and a copy of *Little Women* under the other.

Sarah's parents ran into the water, hanging onto each other like teenagers, shrieking and laughing as tiny swells broke at their waists. Two surfers paddling out to the waves pointed at them and laughed. Sarah's father motioned for her to join them, but she dismissed them with a wave of her hand. Instead, she found a shady spot next to a large rock and opened her book.

"Hi!"

A young girl stood next to the rock, smiling. Her black hair was plaited into two wet braids, and the bright green bathing suit she wore contrasted sharply with her tanned body. She was pretty.

"Hello," Sarah murmured.

"I'm Helen Lane," the girl said, extending her hand. Her palm felt warm and a little sandy. The sweet smell of coconut sunscreen wafted from her skin. "What are you reading?"

"*Little Women*. Have you ever read it?"

"No," Helen lifted a cold clump of sand out of the beach with her toe. "But I've seen the movie. I love Winona Ryder."

Sarah felt suddenly superior to the tanned, pretty girl. "Well, the movie is not nearly as good." Without lifting her eyes from her book, Sarah added, "I'm Sarah Miller, by the way."

Helen seemed unfazed by Sarah's snotty attitude. "Would you like to go bodysurfing later, Sarah?"

"I don't know," Sarah shrugged. "We just moved here. I still haven't unpacked."

Lifting her eyes from her book, Sarah shielded them from the sun. She pretended to be watching a group of surfers paddling out toward the waves.

"Maybe we can go tomorrow," Helen suggested. "You do know how to swim, don't you, Sarah?"

Sarah closed her book. "Of course I know how to swim! It's just that I'm a Midwesterner. I'm not used to the ocean."

Helen studied Sarah's face for a moment, then turned and waved to a man emerging from the water with a surfboard under his arm.

"I gotta go, Sarah. That's my dad. I'll meet you here tomorrow at two o'clock, OK?"

Sarah started to make an excuse, but Helen was already running down the beach toward her father.

Sarah's mother picked up a towel from the sand and draped it over her shoulders. Beads of water flew onto the page of Sarah's book. Sarah sniffed and dried the page with her sleeve.

"Who was that, honey?" her mother asked.

Sarah watched Helen take her father's hand and disappear in a throng of bathers.

"I don't really know," Sarah answered softly, "I guess she's a friend."

By the next morning, Sarah had come up with several excuses why she couldn't go bodysurfing that afternoon. They were so believable, Sarah was intensely pleased with herself: *I left my*

bathing suit in Nebraska. Our new dryer shrank my bikini. My father wants me to see the university. My parents are dragging me up to Disneyland because they think I'll actually enjoy it.

But by the time she met Helen at two, Sarah was so nervous, she'd forgotten them all. "I don't know if I can go swimming, today, Helen," was all she could say. "I feel like I'm going to puke."

"Oh, it's probably just the sun," Helen said. "You'll feel better when you get in the water." Helen touched Sarah's shoulder. "Don't be afraid."

Sarah waded in as far as her knees. She burrowed her toes in the sand and stayed rooted like a tree.

"Are you OK?" Helen asked.

"Yeah, it's just a little cold. I'll get used to it."

The two girls walked out a little farther. Helen dove under a wave. "You have to dive right in, Sarah," she said, surfacing. "It's the only way to get over how cold it is."

Sarah smiled weakly. "I know. It's just that my stomach feels a little funny."

"C'mon, Sarah. It's just like a pool. Only with waves."

Shivering now, Sarah blurted out, "I can't dive in, Helen. I can't swim at all." She looked down into the cold, green water. Her stomach hurt. Helen would never be her friend now that she'd shown herself to be such a coward.

"That's OK." Helen pulled a piece of seaweed from one black braid. "Let's just hang out on the beach."

Sarah and Helen walked to the shore in silence. *She hates me,* Sarah thought. *She'll make some excuse about having to go home.*

She was startled by Helen asking, "Do you want to go to the Snack Shack?" Helen tossed a braid over each shoulder and added, "They have the best onion rings on the beach."

The two girls ordered two boxes of greasy onion rings and two Cokes. They sat down to eat at a wooden picnic table scarred with initials. Helen showed Sarah a little heart she'd carved with the letter *J* in the middle.

"I'm in love with a lifeguard named Jeff Sumrall." Helen leaned over the table and showed Sarah a little gold seahorse charm she wore on a chain. "He gave me this."

"Is he your boyfriend?" Sarah asked, awestruck.

Helen sighed. "I wish." Helen dipped an onion ring into a pool of ketchup. "Jeff's 17. I'm only three years younger than him, but he treats me like I'm this silly little kid."

Sarah confessed she'd never had a boyfriend. "In Nebraska, boys nicknamed me the library mole because I was always inside reading."

Helen was impressed that Sarah had read *Catcher in the Rye*. "I thought only high school kids read that."

"I'm like my father. He's an English professor. He reads everything. My mother says he reads the toothpaste tube while he brushes his teeth."

Helen laughed. "All my dad ever thinks about is surfing."

Helen and Sarah fed the rest of their onion rings to the seagulls. They walked farther down the beach, on the lookout for shells and lost coins.

When the sun started to fall, Helen walked Sarah home, their bare feet burning on the tar road.

Sarah loved visiting the little white beachfront house where Helen lived with her father. Old wooden surfboards and dried puffer fish hung from the ceiling. Each morning that summer, while Helen took surfing lessons from her father, Sarah sat on the beach nearby with her sketch pad or a pile of books. One morning, as Helen was about to follow her father to the water, she said, "I really wish you'd learn to swim, Sarah. Surfing would be so much more fun if you could come out in the water with me."

Sarah blushed. She felt like an old lady sitting on the sand, wearing a floppy hat to keep the sun out of her eyes.

"Lessons start next week over at Marshall High. I'll even take the beginner's class with you so you don't feel alone."

"All right," Sarah relented. After all, if Helen would be there, how bad could it be?

"Miss Miller!" Miss Honora shrieked, leaning over the side of the pool. "You're flopping around like . . . like an octopus!" Miss Honora asked to be addressed as "Ma'am," but Helen had secretly christened her "The Sea Hag."

Despite Helen's opinion of her, Miss Honora had taken an immediate liking to her star pupil. She praised Helen's natural grace in the water. By the second day of class, she'd transferred Helen to the advanced level. "You will never leap like a dolphin if you swim with polliwogs, Miss Lane," she insisted.

Miss Honora's swim class was one of Sarah's worst fears come true. Not only was she the worst swimmer in her class, all the other girls made fun of her frumpy, flowered bathing suit. They whispered to each other when Sarah dog-paddled across the pool because she couldn't master the breaststroke. The more The Sea Hag barked at Sarah to gracefully turn her head and breathe as she swam, the more Sarah gagged and choked on the chlorinated water.

If it wasn't for Helen, waiting for her in the locker room each afternoon, Sarah would have quit The Sea Hag's class after the first day. Helen did her best to cheer up Sarah. That day she removed a water-swollen copy of *Catcher in the Rye* from her purse. "I've been reading a little bit every day after my swim class. I love it."

Even talking about her beloved J. D. Salinger couldn't take Sarah's mind off the weekly nightmare of Miss Honora's class. "I just don't know what the point is, Helen," Sarah moaned. "Even if I pass the class, are you sure I'm ready to swim in the ocean?"

"I'm positive," Helen assured her. "You know how to swim, Sarah. You're just nervous. Besides, I'll be with you."

Three weeks later, when The Sea Hag handed Sarah her Pollywog certification, she and Helen celebrated by going shopping at the U-Save drugstore. Sarah bought herself a set of neon-colored ballpoint pens, two tubes of flavored lip gloss, and a box of Red Hots. Helen purchased a bottle of green nail polish, a mud beauty mask, and a bag of jelly beans. They sat on Helen's front porch and spread out their loot on a small wooden table.

"Do you think Jeff Sumrall would like this color?" Helen asked, wiggling just-dried toes in the air.

"I don't know, Helen," Sarah said, "it's very *Frankenstein*."

"C'mon," Helen slid her feet carefully into her sandals. "Let's go see if Jeff's on duty."

Helen and Sarah raced down to the beach, Sarah's mouth burning from the Red Hots. They rushed up to the lifeguard tower, laughing and stumbling through the sand. Jeff was seated on the tower, listening to the radio and reading a skateboarding magazine. Once he noticed the two girls below, he turned down his radio. "Oh, hey, Helen," he said.

"Hi, Jeff," Helen said breathlessly. She raised her foot and rested it on the lifeguard tower. "What do you think of my toenails, Jeff?"

Jeff grimaced. "Dude, I have to say they look pretty nasty."

Helen giggled, but Sarah was disgusted. How could Helen like someone who called a *girl* dude?

"You ought to be more polite," Sarah said. "For all you know, Helen could be suffering from a rare toenail fungus, *dude*."

"Yeah, Jeff, " Helen added, "for all you know I might have gangrene."

Jeff turned his radio up. "Whatever."

Helen looked at Sarah. They cracked up.

Helen grabbed Sarah's hand. "Bye, Jeff!"

The girls ran laughing into the surf. When the water reached their waists, they stopped running and started swimming. They swam with their heads above water, looking back at Jeff and laughing. Sarah heard The Sea Hag's voice: "You move your arms like an octopus, Miss Miller." She closed her eyes and dove into the water.

A chill ran through Sarah's body at first, but then the water closed around her and it didn't feel cold anymore. Sarah opened her eyes. The water was murky, but she could see the milky soles of Helen's feet ahead of her, kicking up swirls of white water as she swam. Sarah raced up behind her friend and grabbed her leg. Helen whirled around, her eyes wide. The girls surfaced together, taking big breaths of air through their mouths.

"The Sea Hag was right. You are an octopus," Helen joked. "I expected to see suction cup marks on my legs."

Swimming in the ocean wasn't nearly as bad as Sarah imagined. She loved swimming underwater, parting the ocean with her arms. Sometimes it felt as if she was trying to find her way along a hallway in the dark. Other times the sun sent shafts of light through the surface, illuminating tiny fish that rushed along the ocean bottom.

No colored leaves marked the change of seasons in San Diego like they did in Nebraska. But in late August, the morning air felt colder and the scent of eucalyptus trees more pungent.

"Let's go bodysurfing, Sarah." Helen suggested on one of the last days of summer. "The swells aren't going to be too big today. Besides, the water will be way too cold soon to go again."

The early morning mist obscured familiar landmarks on the beach. The Snack Shack and the lifeguard tower looked lonely and abandoned. Helen wore the seahorse necklace Jeff Sumrall had given her. Sarah carried a backpack full of food and Helen's copy of *Catcher in the Rye*. Sarah left the backpack in a cool, dry spot on the big black rock where she and Helen had first met. They walked out to the sea.

"The trick is to let the water carry you," Helen instructed. "But try not to catch the wave too early or you'll get thrashed. Just watch me. I'll take this one, and then you can try the next."

Helen lay flat, waiting for the wave, but it broke too early. The sea lifted Helen up and then gently back down.

Sarah and Helen waited. Another set formed.

"Okay, Sarah. Watch this. I'm just going to let it take me."

Helen turned and paddled toward shore. Sarah watched the wave build behind her. At first Sarah thought the dark shadow that hovered inside the green swell was a mass of seaweed. The sun streamed through the crest of the wave, illuminating the shark floating in the wall of water as if behind glass in an aquarium.

Sarah tried to scream, but her mouth was too dry and tasted like metal. The great white's snout pierced the curve of the water.

Just before the wave sent Sarah spinning through a swirling mass of water, she heard her friend scream.

Drowning seemed a blessing compared with being attacked by a shark. Still, Sarah surfaced in the foamy aftermath. As fast as she could, she swam to where she'd last seen Helen. But her arms and legs felt heavy, the way they did when she tried to run in a dream. Sarah was terrified of seeing the shark again, but even worse was not knowing where it was. She imagined the open mouth, lined with blood, hurtling up from the deep and ripping off her leg.

Sarah spotted Helen clawing her way to the surface, coughing and moaning. Her black hair hung in her face like a curtain of seaweed.

"Don't worry, Helen," Sarah called. "I'm coming."

"It's too late, Sarah."

A triangular fin and sickle-shaped tail rose behind Helen and fell beneath the waves again.

"Helen!" Sarah rushed toward her friend.

Before Helen could answer, her head was jerked violently back into the water. Blood shot out of her mouth as she was yanked beneath the waves. The water turned red. Helen bobbed to the surface again.

The shark let her go, Sarah thought, terrified. *Now it's going to kill me, tear my body into ribbons.* Still, she stayed by Helen. She touched her shoulder. The skin was gouged and tattered. A hunk of flesh came off in her hand. Her friend's arm was bitten off at the elbow. A broken bone gleamed in the water.

Helen's head flopped forward on her chest. She groaned.

Sarah hooked her arm under Helen's ribs. She was glad she couldn't see beneath the dark water. Helen's legs were probably gouged and bleeding. Maybe there was nothing left of them at all. Sarah swam holding her friend's body close.

Sarah never saw the shark again. She only felt a sharp tug accompanied by a rush of water as Helen slipped out from under her arms and into the sea.

Sarah felt most afraid once Helen was gone. Her head pounded. Still, she kept her eyes focused on the shore. *You'll make it*, she told herself, *as long as you don't look back.*

A boat sped toward her, skimming and jumping on the top of the waves. A man leaned out and yelled something to Sarah, but his voice was drowned out by the sound of the outboard motor. It was Jeff Sumrall. His face was ashen. Sarah remembered the gold seahorse Helen had worn around her neck. Jeff leaped into the water and swam toward Sarah. Another man leaned over the side of the boat.

"It's all right, honey" he called, "You're safe. Jeff's got you."

Jeff put his arm around Sarah.

"Are you all right?" he asked.

Sarah realized he didn't even know her name.

"I'm OK," she managed.

"Is . . . Helen . . . " Jeff's voice trailed off.

"She's gone," Sarah whispered.

Jeff and Sarah climbed onboard the boat. Sarah couldn't stop shaking. Jeff gave her a towel to wrap herself in. No one spoke.

Sarah looked back at the ocean, expecting to see a dorsal fin cutting through the waves or Helen waving frantically, *Come back, Sarah. I'm here.* But she saw nothing but water. It was as if nothing out of the ordinary had happened at all. The ocean had healed itself, like a wound.

Sarah Miller was awarded a special medal of bravery by the city of San Diego "for her courageous effort to rescue Helen Lane."

"Do you realize how incredible this is?" Sarah's father said, when he received notification from the city council. "You should be very proud of yourself, Sarah."

It wasn't incredible, Sarah thought. The correct word was *ironic*. Very ironic.

Sarah had became a celebrity overnight. She was invited to dinner at the mayor's mansion. Everyone talked about how excited she must feel about all the attention.

The truth was that Sarah didn't feel anything. It was as if she were out of her body, watching it happen to somebody else.

"I know you're sad, Sarah," her mother said as Sarah prepared for a television interview with Channel 2 news. "But don't you think Helen would be proud of you?"

Sarah shrugged. The makeup man powdered her face. She felt dorky standing there holding a framed certificate of bravery she'd just been awarded by an organization called Young Women Who Dared.

Melanie Moody, the Channel 2 anchorwoman, shook Sarah's hand. "I'm standing here with Sarah Miller, a local heroine who risked her life to save her best friend from the jaws of a killer shark."

The anchorwoman smoothed her helmet of bleached-blond hair. "According to Miss Miller's swim coach, Eunice Honora,

Sarah barely knew how to swim, let alone attempt a rescue maneuver."

Good old Sea Hag, Sarah thought.

Melanie put her hand on Sarah's shoulder as if they were old friends. "I think that makes this story all the more incredible. Would you like to tell our viewers how you became so courageous, Sarah?" the newscaster asked.

"I'm not brave," Sarah replied.

Sarah's mother rolled her eyes. She'd begged Sarah not to give flippant answers on television. A clip of Sarah's speech was going to appear on the national news. Everyone in Nebraska would be watching.

"Now is not the time for false modesty, Sarah," Melanie Moody smiled.

Sarah imagined she and Helen sitting on the front porch of her friend's little white house. It had only been two weeks since they'd treated themselves to presents from the drugstore. Yet that afternoon felt like another lifetime ago.

"Helen was the brave one." Sarah paused. "She was my best friend. When I was with her I was never afraid."

THE LAST PREDATOR

Johnny and Richie Young were brothers all right, but Johnny, just two years older, often teased his younger brother that he was adopted. "That's the only way I can explain your spaciness."

Richie was a straight-A student, founder and president of the Junior Bird-Watchers of Montauk club. Johnny's idea of spending quality time in nature was shooting targets in the woods with his BB gun. Although he took out his aggression on tin cans, he threatened to turn his attention to the bird feeder Richie had built in the backyard. "C'mon, Richie, just a couple of cardinals for practice." Richie could never tell when Johnny was serious. He took down the bird feeder just in case.

Johnny and Richie reacted very differently to their father's death from an attack by a great white, the animal he hoped to champion in the book he was writing, *The Last Predator*. For weeks, Richie couldn't walk into his father's study without breaking down. He used to sit in that same study, poring over Paul Young's zoology texts, asking his father questions about science and animal behavior.

When Johnny saw his brother crying, he'd say, "Do you know what my motto is, Richie? Don't get sad—get even."

The two brothers went to live with their Aunt Grace in Amagansett, farther south along the Long Island coast. "Your father's will specified that the house in Montauk be sold," Aunt Grace explained, "and the money go toward your college education."

It was hard for Richie to leave their home, but he liked Aunt Grace. She could name all the birds that landed in her backyard.

Johnny hated Amagansett. He hitched rides back to Montauk, not returning to Amagansett until dark. Early one August evening, Johnny came into Richie's room and sat on the edge of his bed. Richie thought Johnny was going to tease him about something or other. But Johnny wasn't in a teasing mood.

"Hey Richie," he said. "Remember my other motto?"

"Yeah: Blood is thicker than water."

"That means that no matter what happens, you and me gotta stick together."

"I know, Johnny."

Whenever Johnny asked Richie to swear his undying loyalty, it usually meant he was about to do something stupid, illegal, or both. Like the time he made Richie swear not to tell that he and Jimmy Strand were going to streak the Fourth of July parade.

"You gotta swear, no matter what, you'll *never* sell me out." Johnny was now holding out his hand.

Richie shook it. He can call me a wuss, Richie thought, but he'll never call me a traitor.

"I promise."

"OK," Johnny said. "Here's my plan."

"God knows what kind of trouble he's getting into with those wild friends of his," Aunt Grace lamented one morning as Johnny grabbed a piece of toast from the breakfast table and quickly ran out the door.

"Johnny's friends are OK, Auntie," Richie assured her. "I mean, it's not like they were drug dealers, or thieves, or serial killers, or anything."

"Not yet, anyway," Grace snapped, buttering her toast.

In any case, Johnny wasn't roaming the streets with his teenage friends. He was profiting from the wisdom of great white shark hunter, Whitey Allan. When he returned from Montauk that evening, Johnny was bursting with schemes for revenge.

"So I asked Whitey, what's more likely to kill a white shark: a power head or a regular rifle, a harpoon or a hook? Is it better to nail it right through the gills so it can't breathe, then blow its brains out with a shotgun—"

Richie cocked his head inquisitively. "Meanwhile, the great white is thinking, *Should I bite this guy in half or just rip off his legs?*"

"Hardie har har," Johnny sneered. "For your information, white sharks don't *think*. They're practically retarded." Then he was back talking about Whitey Allen. "He's been shark fishing for 20 years, Richie. And, oh, when I asked him how much he charges to take game fishermen out on boats, he goes, 'Oh, about an arm and a leg.'"

"That's funny." Richie tried to sound interested as he flipped through a copy of *Audubon* magazine.

"You know what Whitey said about Dad?" Johnny imitated Whitey's Maine accent: "'Your father knew a lot about fish for a college guy.'" Richie remembered how their father had always avoided Whitey Allan if they ran into him downtown. "Oh no, he'd say, "here comes Long John Silver."

"You better keep your voice down, Johnny," Richie cautioned. "If Aunt Grace hears you talking about this, she'll have a stroke."

Johnny looked out Richie's bedroom window. "Auntie Grace is out in the garden, brainiac. She can't hear a word I say. Anyway, I made Whitey promise to take you and me out on the boat with him."

Richie groaned. "C'mon, Johnny. I told you before, I'm not into this shark killer thing. Besides, you know I puke if I spend so much as five minutes on a boat."

"What's the real reason?" Johnny sneered. "Are you scared?"

"I'm just not going."

Johnny shook his head "You are such a mega-wuss, Richie. You have a chance to do a really great thing, but you'd rather sit home and bury your face in some lame magazine." Johnny tossed the copy of *Audubon* on the floor.

"Yeah?" Richie snapped. "Maybe you'd actually learn something if *you* read once in a while." Richie reached into his desk drawer and shoved his father's unfinished manuscript into Johnny's hands. "Why don't you find out how Dad would like to be remembered instead of shooting your mouth off like a moron?"

Johnny's face contorted in anger. "Since I'm such a moron, Professor Wuss, why don't *you* go ahead and tell me how our father would like to be remembered?"

Richie hadn't really *read* his father's book, he'd only skimmed the introduction. "For your information, Johnny, great whites aren't exactly my favorite things either. But Dad's whole reason for writing this book was to encourage conservation. The last thing he would want is for his death to inspire people to kill them."

Johnny tossed the manuscript behind his shoulder, scattering the pages all over the floor. "Too bad a moron like me never learned to read."

"I'm sorry I called you a moron." Richie slumped down in his chair. "I didn't mean it."

"I'll be thinking of you when Whitey and I beat your precious shark to death with a crowbar." Johnny slammed the bedroom door behind him, then opened it a crack. "Enjoy your article, Richie. I'm sure it's *fascinating*."

Richie gathered his father's manuscript from the floor. The pages were hard to read, covered as they were with scribbles, arrows, and question marks. Here and there were yellow sticky notes with information his father hadn't had time to integrate into the book. *I could finish it*, Richie thought. *It might take me years, but I could do it*. He lay on his bed and began chapter one:

> The legendary ferocity of *Carcharodon carcharias* begins in the womb. The unborn sharks eat through the uterine walls and devour their weaker brothers and sisters. In a perfect example of the survival of the fittest, only the strongest great whites make the transition from the enclosed fluid of the womb to the open ocean.

If Johnny was an animal, he'd be a great white, Richie reflected, *already ferocious when he came into the world. Born tough.*

When Johnny Young was a little boy, he believed he was Superman. He ran around the yard with a blue towel pinned to his shoulders, a large red *S* drawn on his blue undershirt.

Now that he was almost 16, Johnny felt more like the Invisible Man than the Man of Steel. The more fights he picked or crazy stunts he pulled, the more the bindings of his false self became all you could see of him. If you'd ever unravel the bandages of Johnny's tough-guy personality, there'd be nothing there.

Richie would follow in his father's footsteps and become a great scientist. Johnny imagined that by the time he'd be Whitey Allan's age, he, too, would have scars and wounds crisscrossing his body, each one telling the story of a different adventure, a close call, a brush with death. The faded wound that meandered across Johnny's forehead from a skateboarding accident paled in comparison with the three hundred stitches Whitey'd received after being mauled by a great white in New Jersey.

Johnny half expected Richie to wimp out on him, but he never dreamed the fearless great white shark hunter would turn him down. "You're a good kid, Johnny," Whitey said. "But the truth is, I'm a might older now." Whitey lit a cigarette. "I haven't killed a great white in more'n a few years. It's a terrible thing what happened to your father, but I just can't see riskin' your neck and mine to go out spoilin' for revenge."

If Richie ever found out Whitey refused to go along with him, Johnny would look a bigger failure than he already was. Plan B was more like a last resort than a plan. His name was Kyle Landsman.

Richie once described the 14-year-old as "a few fries short of a Happy Meal." Kyle worshipped Johnny. When Kyle heard that Johnny liked Nirvana, he bought all their CDs. Johnny debated telling Kyle that his new favorite group was the Spice Girls, just to see if Kyle would suddenly become a bubblegum fan.

Kyle may have been a dork, but he'd been sailing his entire life. His parents gave Kyle everything he wanted, including his own boat. The Landsmans were always gone for the weekend, attending weddings and horse shows, leaving Kyle to do whatever he wanted.

Johnny would tell Aunt Grace he'd be spending the weekend at Kyle's house in Montauk. That weekend, he's put his plan—which he would *not* tell Aunt Grace about—into action. Johnny took Kyle out for clam rolls and chocolate shakes early in the week and unveiled his strategy.

"My dad taught me a lot about great whites, Kyle," Johnny lied. "You know, their psychology and everything. Whitey Allan showed me the hands-on part, like, how to kill them. Remember the part in *Jaws* where the guys try to catch the shark by baiting a hook with a pot roast?"

Kyle squeezed a packet of tartar sauce on his clam roll. "I only saw *Jaws 2*."

Johnny tried not to be irritated. "OK, bad example. The point is, a real great white would never go for pot roast. They like tuna and horse meat. I'll make up a batch of chum—you know, that gross stew made of fish guts that attracts sharks. All we need is your boat and your father's shotgun. We'll chum the water off Table Rock Island, wait for Mr. Jaws to show up, then blow his brains out." Johnny made it sound so easy, he'd almost convinced himself.

Kyle stared at his friend, awestruck. "Johnny," he said, "you're the bomb."

Kyle and Johnny started right away preparing for their adventure. Johnny collected a bucket of fish remains from the dock. The local butcher had no horse meat, though. Johnny's chum creation wound up being a beef and fish head stew. Johnny and Kyle hid the buckets in the garage freezer where

Kyle's father used to store venison during deer season. Johnny took Mr. Landsman's rifle and a brand-new hunting knife.

"These too," Kyle said, adding a box of Twinkies on the pile of weapons. "The ocean air always makes me hungry."

Friday night, Johnny was walking out the door on his way to Montauk when Richie said, "Hold on, Johnny." He stepped out onto the front porch, closing the door behind him. Richie wore his jacket and carried a small duffel bag.

"I've changed my mind," Richie whispered. "I want to come with you."

Johnny shook his head. "I already told Whitey you weren't coming. He said it was just as well. The boat is kind of small, and he doesn't want to have to waste time mopping up your barf—"

"I'm worried about you, Johnny."

"Well, don't be." Johnny turned to go.

"Come on," Richie pleaded. "Stay home. We'll order pizza and work on Dad's book. I need your help, really—"

Johnny shot Richie one of his "death" looks.

"No thanks, Professor."

It was a warm, cloudless morning when Kyle and Johnny set out for Table Rock Island. From the time they left the dock until they reached the island, Kyle assaulted Johnny with questions about great whites: How big do they get? Which do they like better, warm water or cold? Will they try to eat our boat?

As they neared Table Rock, Johnny hauled the two plastic buckets of chum toward the side of the boat. He gagged as he pulled off the plastic lid. The gory mixture smelled even more rotten having thawed. Blood splashed on the leather seats of the boat as he hoisted the bucket over the side.

"Dude," Kyle said, stuffing a Twinkie in his mouth, "that's new upholstery."

"Perhaps if you'd assist me, I wouldn't be spilling this nasty stuff all over the yacht," Johnny said in a fake British accent.

Kyle lifted the pail over the side. "Sorry, Johnny."

"We'll wait a while before we dump the other one," Johnny said, retrieving a can of soda and a comic book from his jacket. "Until then, I'll thrill to the adventures of *Ironman*."

While Johnny and Kyle sailed across the open sea, Richie knelt in the grass of Aunt Grace's backyard, pulling weeds.

As he ripped their roots from the dirt, lines from *The Last Predator* drifted through his head, like: *The hypothesis that great whites disable their prey with an initial attack, then wait for the animal to bleed to death before consuming it, does not account for those unfortunate victims who are bitten in half or swallowed whole.*"

Johnny would be OK, Richie told himself. When his brother was three, he'd almost drowned in a neighbor's swimming pool. Last summer, he'd been hit by a car while skateboarding. There was blood all over the road, but he walked away with a few stitches. Richie remembered his father's words as they all drove home from the emergency room: *Son, you must have a guardian angel.*

Richie swept a pile of weeds into a garbage bag and hauled a bag of bird feed from the toolshed. Aunt Grace plopped down onto a lawn chair and removed her gardening gloves. "I hope that Kyle Landsman has at least an ounce of common sense," she said.

"Don't worry," Richie replied, pouring seed carefully into the top of the feeder. "I'd say he has at least an ounce."

"The last thing Johnny needs is someone to encourage his wild side." Aunt Grace shook her head. "When I think of the things that boy pulls, it's a miracle he's still alive."

Richie watched a cardinal land on a branch above the feeder. He closed his eyes and said a silent prayer for his brother.

Sharks are like cops, Johnny thought. When you really need them, they're never around. He and Kyle had been out on the ocean four hours without having seen so much as a fin. Johnny managed to overlook Kyle's irritating personality until the young Landsman accidentally threw their sandwiches overboard while trying to dump melted ice from the cooler. Johnny tried to satisfy his hunger with Twinkies, but the spongy snacks tasted exactly like the fishy chum stench that filled the air.

"I think I'm getting a sunburn," Kyle whined. "Can we go in soon?"

Johnny summoned his last shred of patience. "Remember, Kyle. The only reason those shark shows on the Discovery Channel look exciting is because they edit out all the boring parts," he said. "Let's go to the lagoon and dump the rest of this slop."

Table Rock looked lonely and cold, its black rocks streaked with bird excrement. As they neared the island, Johnny noticed a net wrapped tightly around an outcropping of rock. A few yards away, a tangled mass of filament rose from the water.

"There's a dolphin or something stuck in the net over there, Kyle. Let's go check it out."

Kyle guided the boat closer. The hair on Johnny's neck stood on end. The shark was at least a foot longer than Kyle's 15-foot boat. Scars and faint traces of blood covered its snout, but the fish looked more weary than menacing. The deep charcoal color of its head gave way to an eerie, glowing white beneath its jaw. The wholly black eye stared at Johnny. Johnny wondered how anything could look so scary and so beautiful at the same time. The shark probably weighed over three thousand pounds, with rows of teeth as sharp as knives, yet trapped in the net, it looked defenseless, even fragile.

"Should I get the rifle?" Kyle whispered excitedly.

"No," Johnny said. "Just wait a minute."

"How do you think it got trapped, Johnny?"

"These nets look invisible underwater. Maybe it was swimming to the chum slick and swam right into it." Johnny looked at the bound fish, suspended in the water. "Probably the more he tried to break free, the more tangled he got."

"He's pretty awesome, isn't he?" Kyle said.

"Yeah." Johnny turned to retrieve the hunting knife. "He's also gonna die."

Kyle put his hand on Johnny's shoulder. "Hey, Johnny, don't you think you should try to shoot it, first?"

"Even I wouldn't be so low as to kill a *captive* animal, Kyle." Johnny removed the knife from its leather sheath. "I'm gonna cut the net so he can get outta here." *Watch the shark thank me by ripping my head off*, Johnny thought glumly. *Headless Johnny Young, number one shark conservationist in the world.*

"Dude, don't get eaten," Kyle said.

Johnny leaned out over the side of the boat. "Thanks for the brilliant advice, Kyle." He slid the knife under several strands wound tightly around the shark's head. The filaments snapped easily beneath the sharp blade. The shark thrashed its head free, snapping its jaw and rolling its black eyes, soaking the boys with water. It bucked and twisted its body like a rodeo bronc but remained tethered to the rock.

"I have to cut the rest of the net, Kyle."

"I can't bring the boat in there, Johnny." Kyle studied the narrow corridor of water between the rocky crags. "It would get nailed on the rocks. We'd sink or get stuck for sure." Kyle handed Johnny his father's shotgun. "You're gonna have to let it drown or put it out of its misery."

Johnny measured the distance from the boat to the rock. *Ten seconds,* he told himself. *I can make it to the rock in ten seconds. Stay calm; swim with smooth, even strokes. Ten seconds.*

Before he could talk himself out of it, Johnny took off his T-shirt and shoes. *I'm about to risk my life to free a shark that probably killed my father and would bite me in half given the chance,* Johnny thought. *I'm not a moron—I'm an idiot.*

Johnny Young stood in the middle of Kyle Landsman's boat in his black nylon shorts, holding the hunting knife between his teeth, like a pirate. He slipped over the side of the boat. The water was freezing. Johnny took a deep breath and swam toward the rocks.

"Johnny! Johnny! Come back!" Kyle called after him. "You're insane!"

Adrenaline surged through Johnny's body. He kept his eyes fixed on the rocks. The shark's tail whipped back and forth.

"Easy now, Mr. Jaws," Johnny sputtered, "I'm just here to help you."

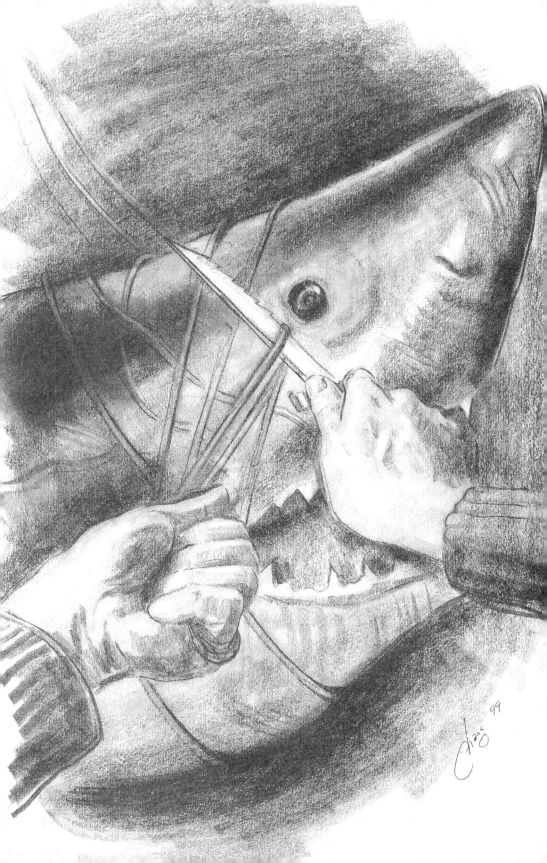

Johnny wrapped one arm around the rocks and pulled himself out of the water. Clinging tightly to the rock with one arm, he took his knife from between his teeth. Then he sawed through the strands that bound the shark to the rocks. *This blade is like his teeth*, Johnny considered. *Sharp and clean, slices right through skin, muscle, bone . . .*

"Hurry, Johnny," Kyle called. "It looks half dead."

Johnny drove the knife through the taut fibers. The net drooped and fell into the water like a dew-heavy spiderweb onto grass. Johnny felt euphoric. It was as if some hard knot inside his chest had dissolved. The shark was free. It did not swim away but hovered there in the sea. "Don't die on me," Johnny said softly, "not after all that."

The shark slipped underwater. The fin surfaced a few feet from Kyle's boat. Kyle picked up the shotgun.

"I'm sorry, Johnny," Kyle shouted. "I just can't handle this."

"Wait!" Johnny yelled. "Don't shoot!"

Kyle trained the gun unsteadily on the black dorsal fin. The shark sank below the waves.

Kyle lowered the gun reluctantly.

The boys stared at each other. The world was silent, except for the screeching cries of sea birds circling in the sky above the island.

The shark appeared again, keeping its snout above the water as it cruised toward the rocks.

"No need to thank me," Johnny said, "No need at all." Johnny clung to the wet, jagged rocks the way he and Richie used to wrap themselves around the maple trees in their backyard. Johnny's limbs ached. Cold fear shot through his veins as the shark circled the rock. *He's waiting for me to get tired and fall into the water*, he realized. Then, with a thrash of its tail, the shark turned and swam toward the open sea.

"Keep an eye on him, Kyle," Johnny called.

Kyle tracked the fish's movement through a pair of binoculars. "Kyle? Where'd he go?"

"I—I think he's gone," Kyle stammered. "But I don't know."

Johnny's arms and legs were stiff. The short distance between the rocks and the boat looked like the English channel. *If I was going to die, I would have already*, he reasoned.

Johnny let go of the rock and fell into the water. It seemed like an eternity passed before he felt Kyle's hand pulling him onboard. Johnny sat, his chest heaving, dripping sea water all over Kyle's new upholstery. *Quite an adventure*, Johnny mused, *without a scar to show for it.*

"What do you do for an encore, dude?" Kyle asked, handing him a towel. "Alligator wrestling?"

"Nothing," Johnny breathed. "Let's go home. I'm hungry."

On Sunday, Richie was sitting at his computer when he heard the front door slam.

"Honey!" Johnny called, "I'm home!"

Richie had spent the day imagining horrific scenes: Johnny holding onto Whitey's hand as he slid into the bloody jaws of a great white. Johnny on a stretcher being loaded into an ambulance, a shredded stump of flesh and bone where his right leg had been.

But Johnny Young had survived again. He ran up the stairs to his brother's room with all his limbs and sarcasm intact, carrying a bag of sandwiches from the Village Sub Shop.

"Johnny!" Richie cried. "You're alive! And you've brought lunch!" Johnny handed Richie a roast beef sandwich. "It's a long story. Let's eat first."

Johnny described all the events that made up the story, but it was hard for him to put into words everything that happened there at Table Rock. Johnny Young only knew that for the first time in his life, he felt free.

"There's something about staring into a great white's eyes." Johnny finished his Coke. "It's like nothing in the world will ever seem so scary or so awesome again."

Richie nodded. "That shark would have died without your help, Johnny. Dad would be proud of you," he said. "But I still don't understand—what happened to your blood plan for revenge."

Johnny shook his head. "I don't know, Richie. Maybe I'm just a big wuss after all."

"I'm the wuss, Johnny," Richie smiled. "You're the moron."

SHARK SENSE

Thirteen-year-old Lisa Jordan knew exactly what she wanted to do with her life. "I will be the world's number one expert on great white sharks," Lisa replied without hesitation when her seat mate on the plane from Sydney to Port Lincoln, Australia—an older woman named Margaret—asked her what she wanted to be when she grew up.

"That's quite an ambition for a young girl," Margaret beamed.

Lisa could tell by Margaret's faint smile that the older woman didn't take her seriously. Lisa didn't mind. She'd read somewhere that scientific geniuses were always misunderstood in their own lifetime. Lisa was already enduring taunts of "Hey, Shark Girl" and "If you love great whites so much, why don't you marry one?" from kids at school. In sixth grade, someone had taped a picture of a great white with a bloody mouth on Lisa's desk, with the words PLEASE KISS ME written on it.

The only person who understood Lisa's passion was her Uncle Ray. Ray was an adventurer. Lisa's family hadn't seen him since he left their hometown of Nutley, New Jersey, to travel the world. Ray's postcards described diving with hammerhead sharks in Mexico and traveling to the Solomon Islands, where the native people made him an honorary shark priest. Now Ray had settled in Australia, where he'd devoted his life to studying great whites.

"I've come to Australia to go on an expedition with my Uncle Ray, called Project Great White," Lisa said to Margaret, removing from her bag a stack of snapshots Ray had sent. "This is my uncle, and these are the other two researcher guys, Dr. Barlowe and Dr. Merchant. Those rocks in the background are the Triton Islands, where their ship is moored."

While Margaret flipped through the pictures, Lisa went on excitedly about Project Great White.

"The South Australian Marine Society thinks the great white population has declined, so they've hired experts to attract and tag the sharks. Uncle Ray says he's tagged about five so far. One was close to 20 feet long. Uncle Ray was leaning over the edge of the boat, trying to stick a tag under the shark's dorsal fin, when it jumped right out of the water and snapped a chunk of horse meat from the bait line, like it was a potato chip."

Margaret shook her head and handed Lisa back the photographs. "Your uncle is an incredibly brave man. I was afraid to take a bath after I saw *Jaws*."

Lisa laughed. "Uncle Ray *is* brave." She stared at the picture. "I guess he's the only person in the world I *really* admire."

Uncle Ray was waiting for Lisa by the baggage claim, pushing a toothpick between his lips. He wore a faded blue jacket and held a tattered piece of cardboard with her name written inside a drawing of a black dorsal fin. Lisa waved and ran toward him.

"I made this sign to make sure you'd recognize me," Ray announced, taking her suitcase. Lisa hugged her uncle. Ray's tanned face was covered with faint lines, like a folded piece of paper. He smelled vaguely of cigarettes, fish, and gasoline.

"You look exactly like your photo," Lisa said, tugging on her uncle's sleeve. "Only I pictured you wearing one of those cool Project Great White jackets like Merchant and Barlowe have."

Ray smiled weakly. "I must have left mine on the ship."

"It's still light," Lisa said as they walked out of the small airport terminal into the cool sea air of Port Lincoln. "Do you think we have time to head out to the boat?"

"Why don't we grab some dinner instead?" Ray suggested. "We'll have plenty of time tomorrow onboard the *Skate*."

Plenty of time? Lisa would only be onboard the boat for three days. Besides, who could think about eating in some corny seafood restaurant when there were white sharks cruising the ocean only a mile from shore?

Ray took Lisa to a dark, chilly restaurant called The White Pointer. A set of jaws hung over the entrance. The only light came from a brightly lit aquarium filled with yellow and blue fish.

"You know why they call it the White Pointer, don't you?"

"It's the Australian term for white shark," Lisa said, glancing at the menu. "That's pretty basic, Uncle Ray."

Ray smiled. "I guess I forgot who I was talking to."

Sitting in The White Pointer, eating hamburgers and cokes, made Lisa feel like a child her uncle was trying to entertain. Couldn't he see how eager she was to begin their adventure?

Over dinner, Ray asked Lisa questions about her long flight from New Jersey, and how her mother was. Lisa didn't want to be rude, but her excitement about being in Port Lincoln made everything seem like an annoying distraction. Finally, she asked, "Have you seen any more sharks since that 20-footer who snapped the bait line?"

Ray stirred his coke with his straw. It reminded Lisa of something a nervous kid would do, not a grown man.

"Did I say 20 feet?" Ray questioned. "I might have been off just a little in my estimation. But to answer your question, no, we never saw him again."

"I think you told me that shark was a female," Lisa corrected gently. "Remember? It had mating scars on its back? The male was the one who had his eyeball ripped out by the sea lion."

"That's right. Now I remember. Holy smokes, Lisa. With your memory, you won't need to keep a field notebook on your expeditions."

"I just hope I can be as brave as you, Uncle Ray. I can't imagine leaning over the side of the boat and having to stick a tag right under a shark's fin."

"It's really no big deal," Ray said, removing a wad of cash from his wallet. "I mean, you get used to it."

"I think you should write a book about all the things you've done. I read your postcards about a zillion times."

"Well, that's kind of you to say, Lisa, but Merchant and Barlowe are the real heroes of this project." Ray retrieved a cigarette from his jacket pocket.

"Don't be modest, Uncle Ray. You went to school. I'm sure you know just as much about white sharks as they do."

"What I don't know," Ray said, exhaling a cloud of smoke, "could fill a book."

As they drove along the dusty beach road back to her uncle's house, Lisa gazed out at the Indian Ocean and imagined a huge ghost-white fish cruising parallel to the land, its fin rising and falling in the dark water.

Ray's small beach cottage was cluttered with travel guides to exotic countries, old volumes of ocean mythology, and stacks of books on sharks. Lisa stayed up most of the night, trying to overcome her jet lag by reading about sharks. She thought about asking to borrow Ray's copy of *Myth or Maneater*, but who would have time to read with all the excitement onboard the *Skate*?

Ray woke up Lisa at five-thirty in the morning. He made two cups of muddy instant coffee and loaded the bright yellow Zodiac raft full of food and diving gear.

"How come you need to bring all that stuff?" Lisa asked, stepping inside the outboard.

"Oh, I just promised the guys I'd pick up a few things," Ray replied awkwardly.

The sky mirrored the deep blue color of the ocean as the little boat skittered toward the Triton Islands. Lisa spent the hour-long journey making a chart in her diary to record her great white sightings. As a scientist, Lisa needed to remember everything: the time of day, the approximate temperature of the air and water, whether the sea was choppy or smooth. She loaded film in her camera and cleaned the lenses of the binoculars her father had given her as a birthday present.

As the Zodiac rounded a rocky corner of the largest of the Triton Islands, Lisa could see the *Skate* moored about a hundred yards from shore. Her heart thudded in her chest. *Calm down*, she told herself. *You don't want to look like a total spaz in front of scientists.*

Barlowe appeared at the edge of the boat as Ray guided his outboard up to the stern. "Thank God, my junk food supply is here!" he exclaimed. "Merchant ate the last chocolate bar yesterday, and I almost murdered him."

"I brought everything," Ray assured him. "Candy bars, coffee—I even picked up those camera lenses you ordered."

Barlowe helped Lisa climb up the metal ladder on the side of the boat. "You must be Lisa," he smiled. "Ray says you are the great white's number one fan. Maybe you will do me the honor of describing one to me? It's been so long since I've seen one

I've practically forgotten what they look like." Barlow smiled weakly.

Lisa looked confused.

"What about the 20-footer?" she asked. "The one that bit through a 30-pound piece of horse meat like it was a potato chip?"

"Potato chips!" Barlowe cried, only half hearing her. "Did you bring any potato chips, Ray?"

"Yes, Barlowe," Ray nodded, his face flushed with embarrassment. "Why don't you show Lisa around the ship while I unpack all this."

Barlowe and Lisa made their way across the deck of the *Skate*, which was cluttered with coils of rope, blood-stained plastic buckets, and an unassembled steel shark cage.

"I thought you guys would have one of those clear diving cylinders made of bullet-proof plastic," Lisa said, gesturing to the cage.

Barlowe raised his eyebrows. "We don't quite have the Cousteau Society's budget, my dear, but I'm impressed with your taste."

Barlowe and Lisa descended to a tiny room below deck. The table was crowded with computer monitors and ultrasonic transmitters used to track the movements of sharks. Dr. Merchant sat at a wooden table covered with maps, entering information into the glowing screen of his laptop. Lisa cringed, remembering her hand-drawn chart.

Merchant shook Lisa's hand and glanced at his watch. "I'm glad Ray's here. It's about time to chum. I can't tell you how invaluable your uncle has been to us on this project, Lisa."

"Most guys wouldn't do this kind of work for *money*," Barlowe added. "Ray has worked like a dog for free. We haven't seen a white shark for the entire time we've been at the Tritons, but Ray keeps us entertained telling us all those tall tales about his adventures in the South Pacific." Barlowe winked at Lisa as if she was in on the joke.

"How he has time to mop the deck and ladle fish guts between making all those deliveries is beyond me," Merchant sighed.

"Deliveries?" Lisa questioned.

Barlowe stared at Lisa. "Your uncle works for the Marine Society, delivering supplies to the different research stations. You knew that, right?"

"Yeah, of course. I was just confused for a minute."

Lisa pretended to examine a map of the Indian Ocean while she let Barlowe's words sink in. Ray had lied about everything. He probably made up the story of the 20-foot shark to entertain himself while he mopped fish guts from the deck. *My uncle the adventurer*, Lisa thought, bewildered, *is nothing but a janitor*.

Barlowe broke the awkward silence. "Maybe we should let Merchant finish his work. Why don't you give me a hand getting the bait lines ready, Lisa?"

When Lisa and Barlowe emerged on deck, Ray was dumping frozen fish heads into a bucket of horse blood. Ray tried to catch Lisa's eyes as he shoveled the bloody slop over the side of the boat. Lisa turned and followed Barlowe to the other side of the deck where he removed a large plywood silhouette of a sea lion from a storage closet.

"We don't have the see-through cage, although the Marine Society did spring for this delightful decoy."

"I saw one of these fake seals on the Discovery Channel," Lisa said. "Some scientists cast both the fresh bait *and* the surface shape to see which one the shark will attack first." Barlowe retrieved a bucket of whale blubber from the freezer and smeared the oily goop on the decoy. The sour smell made Lisa gag.

"Ah, yes, the old sight versus smell hypothesis. Common sense tells me this is the perfect white shark magnet," Barlowe said, attaching a tether to the silhouette and tossing it into the sea. "But common sense isn't the same as shark sense."

Lisa and Barlowe sat on folding chairs, eating candy bars and watching the surface shape drift in the water. The thick red cloud of chum on the surface was occasionally broken up by schools of silver tommy ruffs, but no sharks.

Lisa felt a sudden need to impress Barlowe. "I think the most amazing thing about sharks is that even without being able to see or smell their prey they can still detect its electromagnetic impulses using the Ampullae of Lorenzini."

"True. Even if they can't see you or smell you, they can still find you."

"I want to be like that guy Lorenzini," Lisa continued, licking melted chocolate off her fingers. "I want to discover something about great whites that no one has ever known about before."

Barlowe sighed. "Well, good luck to you, Lisa. I've been studying white sharks for 15 years, and I still can't tell you where they breed or how big their young are. I can't tell you about their migration patterns or why it is we've been serving an all-you-can-eat buffet in some of the most shark-infested waters of the world and haven't seen a single fin."

Lisa was silent. She remembered a classmate jeering, "There's a difference between being an expert and acting like a know-it-all." Lisa saw Ray approaching and buried her face in her journal.

"I'm heading to the upper deck for watch duty, Barlowe," Ray said, wiping the sweat from his forehead with one blood-stained hand. "You ought to come up with me and see the view, Lisa."

"No, thanks," she muttered, staring at her empty shark-sighting chart.

The afternoon seemed to stretch on forever. The stench of blood and fish guts hung in the air. Lisa rubbed lotion onto her sunburned shoulders. Barlowe seemed more interested in watching a soccer match on the battery-powered TV than talking about sharks. Although she would never have admitted it, Lisa had begun to feel seasick. When the sun went down, she skipped the fish dinner Merchant had prepared, crawled into her bunk, and went to sleep.

Ray left the next morning to make a delivery to a team of sea lion researchers on one of the Tritons. Barlowe cast out the bait lines and disappeared below deck to work with Merchant. Hours passed. Lisa started to wonder if there were any great white sharks left in the entire world. Ray returned in the early afternoon. He gave his niece a sheepish wave and ascended to his watch station. Lisa was about to sneak away to the bathroom and search for seasickness pills when she heard the clang of the bell on the upper deck.

Lisa grabbed her binoculars. Barlowe and Merchant rushed to the stern. Ray hurried down the ladder. "Do you see it? Swimming right toward the surface target?"

Another 20-footer, perhaps, Lisa thought bitterly.

Lisa watched the dorsal side of the shark skim the bloody surface. The animal was only five feet long and looked more brown than gray. It touched one flipper of the fake seal, fell beneath the scarlet murk, and was gone.

Merchant and Barlowe debated the identity of the mystery shark for the rest of the afternoon. Soupfin. Spiny dogfish. Immature bronze whaler.

Ray lit a cigarette. "Well, whatever it was," he said mournfully, "it's gone now."

The next morning, Merchant announced they'd decided to leave the Tritons a day early.

"I think it's time for us to try our luck in the open ocean," Merchant said. "We sure aren't making much progress here."

Lisa didn't know what she dreaded more, the flight home to New Jersey without having seen a great white or the trip back to the mainland with her uncle.

Lisa and Ray said their good-byes to Merchant and Barlowe and climbed into the Zodiac. Barlowe gave Lisa one of his precious chocolate bars to eat on the trip back. Lisa waved to the scientist until the *Skate* was out of sight. Then she turned to face her uncle.

"Merchant loaned me his boogie board," Ray enthused. "I thought maybe you'd want to go bodysurfing. There's this really great beach on Commonwealth Island. Kids from Port Lincoln surf there all the time."

Lisa nodded. They sailed on in silence. When Ray saw the island in the distance, he turned off the outboard and seated himself at the oars.

"Lisa, I know I shouldn't have made up all that stuff about being a researcher," Ray explained, "but your mother would never have let you come on this trip if she thought I was still just . . . you know . . . a drifter."

"But you could have told *me* the truth," Lisa said sullenly.

"I tried to tell you, but . . . the real truth is, Lisa, I never had the discipline it takes to become a marine biologist." Ray's eyes narrowed. "I've never done a brave thing in my life, Lisa. I made everything up, and I'm sorry. But you're different. You can do anything you want to do. You can be anybody you want to be." Uncle Ray looked down. "I'm sorry, Lisa. Let me make it up to you. . . ." A gentle swell lifted the Zodiac up in the water. The shark's triangular head rose stealthily out of the water behind Ray. Neither he nor Lisa saw it at first. "I want you to be the best shark researcher—"

"Uncle Ray! Look out!" Lisa cried. The fish closed its jaws around the motor, flipping the Zodiac over on its side. Bags of food and bottled water bounced across Lisa's legs before falling into the ocean. Then, as suddenly as the raft had tipped, it righted itself, landing with a wet slap on the water.

"Lisa, my God, are you OK?" Ray asked frantically. Blood trickled down from a cut on his forehead. The outboard hung crookedly from the side of the raft.

"Yes." Lisa paused. "But I hear something hissing." A strange sense of calm overtook her. "I think the shark tore a hole in the raft."

Ray turned around. He leaned over the side and retrieved the boogie board that was slowly floating out to sea. "Take this," he ordered, tossing the board to Lisa. "Swim to the island as fast as you can."

A tall, ragged dorsal fin appeared above the lapping swells.

"Now!" Ray screamed. "Don't wait for me!"

Lisa gripped the board and threw herself into the water. With a few fast kicks, she propelled herself from the wreckage. When she looked over her shoulder, she saw Ray slamming an oar into the white shark's eye. The thrashing fish sank beneath the surface. Ray began to swim in Lisa's direction, arms chopping through the water.

"Swim, Lisa, swim!" Ray yelled before the shark pulled him down with a violent jerk. Lisa saw him go under.

She knew there was very little she could do. Her breath came in short gasps as she turned away from the attack and began kicking toward shore, her eyes filled with tears.

Lisa's legs scissored through the water as her fingernails dug into the foam board. What did the books say? Thrash. Scream. Poke them in the eyes. Barlowe's words returned to her: *Even if they can't see you or smell you, they can still find you.*

Waves were forming and breaking off a sandbar about a hundred yards from the shore of the island. *If I can make it that far,* Lisa reasoned, *I'll let the waves carry me in.* She kept her eyes focused on the sandbar, afraid of what she might see if she looked below into the murky water. The shark could easily mistake her for a seal, hurtle up from below, and grab her before she had time to scream. For the first time in her life, Lisa wished she didn't know so much about the behavior of great white sharks.

The ocean had been slick with blood for days and no shark had appeared. What had attracted it now? *Common sense is not the same as shark sense.*

Lisa imagined the different ways she could die: *The shark might take a bite and wait for me to bleed to death, pull off my leg below the knew, or crush me, biting me in half. Or maybe,* Lisa thought grimly, *the shark won't attack at all. Maybe it's no longer hungry.*

Lisa had almost reached the sandbar when the great white rammed into the bottom of her boogie board, tossing her straight into the center of a breaking wave. She flipped upside

down in the greenish water. Pebbles and strands of seaweed flew around her, going up her nose and into her mouth.

Fear infused her arms and legs with superhuman energy. She sped through the foamy wake toward her board. One or two large waves would dump her on the shore of the island, she was sure. Lisa gripped her board and quickly paddled toward the set of swells.

As she rose on the crest of a wave, a black hole ringed with white teeth rushed toward her through the curved wall of water. She made one blind, violent kick that connected with the shark's nose, and then folded her legs toward her back. Any minute she would feel the jaws clamp down around her waist. Would she feel pain or just pressure?

From the top of the breaker, Lisa saw the sharp curved fin slice the surface of the water ahead of her. The wave would break, propelling her either onto the shark's back or into its mouth. She made one last effort to swim against the tide, toward the open sea, but a swirling surge of water overcame her, hurling her toward the shallows. The shark's rough skin grazed her legs as the wave propelled her past the fish and dumped her in the tidal break.

Lisa crawled along the shoreline on her hands and knees, then rose slowly to her feet. Salt water blurred her vision. She stumbled forward, coughing up snot and sea water.

Even as she felt the hard, cold sand beneath her feet, she imagined a huge wave hurling the shark through the air, its jaws snapping wildly as it landed on the shore, grabbing her leg and dragging her back into the sea. When she no longer felt the tide wash over her ankles, Lisa dared to turn around. The white had vanished in the crashing surf.

A blond boy in black swim trunks was running down the beach toward her. "The kids from Port Lincoln surf there all the time," Uncle Ray had said. *Uncle Ray?* Was he really gone?

He had saved her life.

Another boy stood on the rocks farther up the beach. He was shading his eyes with his hand and pointing to Lisa. He seemed as far away as Barlowe had been when he'd waved good-bye to her from the bow of the *Skate*.

"Hey, are you all right?" the boy asked. He pointed at the raw patch of skin on Lisa's calf. "What happened? Did you get scraped against a rock or something?"

Lisa didn't answer. For the first time in her life, Lisa Jordan felt like she knew absolutely nothing.